About the Author

Born in Barnstaple, raised in Bristol. She studied Animals most of her life, but her true love is writing. If it wasn't for her family and friends, she wouldn't be who she is now. A dreamer. Other than writing her biggest dream to open a pub or a café.

One Moment

K. G. Snow

One Moment

Olympia Publishers
London

www.olympiapublishers.com
OLYMPIA PAPERBACK EDITION

A CIP catalogue record for this title is
available from the British Library.

ISBN: 978-1-80074-346-5

This is a work of fiction.
Names, characters, places and incidents originate from the writer's
imagination. Any resemblance to actual persons, living or dead, is
purely coincidental.

First Published in 2024

Olympia Publishers
Tallis House
2 Tallis Street
London
EC4Y 0AB

Printed in Great Britain

Dedication

I dedicate this to all my friends and family. I love you all.
Thank you. In loving memory of Dominic and Great Aunty
Chris

Acknowledgements

Mum, Dad, Anna, Great Aunty Chris and Grandma. Thank you so much for supporting me and putting up with me constantly; I wouldn't be anywhere without my family. As for my friends who are like my family – Becky, Shoni, Emily, Ella, Megan, Tianna, Laura, Alice, Nicole, Tracey, Nicola, Valerie and Simon – thank you for supporting me, encouraging me, and being there for me. I also acknowledge many other friends who I have not named. You have been a massive help and I also thank you. You know who you are and I love you all so very much. Finally, I'd like to thank Mrs Crowsley, an English teacher who helped me in school and encouraged me to be my best. Thanks to you, I have accomplished a lot in my life. I have already thanked you, but I want to thank you again. You're an amazing teacher and it was an honour to have been taught by you.

Chapter 1

In London sits The Astro, owned by the newspaper named after it. The building is forty floors tall and is home to different offices. However, the thirtieth floor is home to the newspaper which is full of stories of people, business updates, weather, fashion, and news collected around the country.

One of its best loved reporters is thirty-five year old Dominic Wolf. He is six foot two of perfection. His dark brown hair is short and spikey but soft like velvet, and always in perfect condition. His deep blue eyes are always looking for the truth and the brighter side of life. He interviews celebrities but never pries into their private life, which is rare for most newspaper and magazine reporters.

Dominic is one of the best writers in the business; he wins awards for articles and dedicates them to the people he works with, such as Levi, his life partner, and Colin, one of his best friends. But, recently, he has been losing his touch. His articles are becoming destructive and vicious. It seems like the Dominic Wolf everyone once loved has all but vanished. What's left is the grief-stricken man, baring his teeth at the country.

"Where is Wolf?" shouts the chief editor. Her yell echoes over the noise of the office and silence falls. The chief editor stands in front of her office wearing high-waisted jeans and a dark blue blouse with silver buttons, accessorised by a simple necklace. Ashley Moretti is the chief editor, and stands amongst the strongest business women in the country.

11

Colin is making a cup of coffee in the kitchen area tucked away in a corner of the office. He pokes his head out, his curly, unruly hair bounces as he moves to look at his stunned and silent colleagues. He chuckles slightly as he looks back at the furious Ashley Moretti.

"Out of office," he calls back to her with a slight smile as he returns to finish making his coffee.

"Out of office? Well, tell him that he needs to come and see me as soon as he graces us with his presence!" Still furious, Ashley returns to her office. Her office is one of those swanky ones surrounded by glass, not walls. Documents can be seen lying open on tables, whilst others are neatly stacked. Ashley is a hard worker and from the moment she became Chief Editor, nothing changed the priceless respect she received from her colleagues. Colin nodded holding in a smirk that threatened to escape

"I don't know how you do it, Colin," Miles exclaims. Miles is the kind of man who always has a few coffee stains on his paperwork.

"Do what?" Colin replies, sipping his coffee whilst leaning against the entrance of the kitchen.

"Handle the boss like that. I always find it hard to approach her," Miles says, nodding his head towards her office.

Colin laughs slightly. "You know, Miles, she's really nice. She's a hard worker just like us. Ashley just gets a little fired up at work." Colin smiles to himself as he watches her placing different articles and images together on a whiteboard.

"Huh?" Miles looks confused. Colin blinks and looks at Miles, who shakes his head and says, "It doesn't matter. I better be getting back to work."

Colin is one of the other reporters at The Astro and is

12

Dominic's best friend. The two make an unbeatable team. Colin's green eyes are also always searching for truth and his demeanour is gentle, making him easy to approach. However, no one should be fooled; the pen is mightier than the sword, which suits Colin's personality very, very well.

Dominic sits outside a café watching people walking past him on their phones and tablets, their ears blocked with headphones as they go about their morning.

"Here you are, Mr Wolf. Your Danish with a cherry, one tea with a dash of milk, and a vanilla coffee is ready," the elderly lady tells him with a smile.

Dominic smiles back and says, "Thank you, Mrs M. Perfect as always." Mrs M laughs out loud as she touches his shoulder.

"Off with you. Otherwise, you'll be late for work and I won't have any room for paying customers," Mrs M says, telling him off. Laughing, Dominic takes the bag and cup holder and begins his journey through the morning foot traffic.

Entering The Astro, Dominic has an obvious popularity as he's called to by passing people; he says hello to the receptionists and the security guard calls out, "Morning, Wolf." Dominic nods, giving them a smile in return.

As Dominic walks towards the lift, he feels his chest tightening and his breathing quicken. As he presses the button to call the lift, under his breath he whispers, "I can do it today. I can do it today." As the doors open, he hesitates before stepping into the lift, his vision wavering slightly, forcing him to hold his arm out to steady himself.

Closing his eyes, Dominic feels a hand gently touch his, and his breathing returns to normal. Opening them, Dominic pushes a button luminous with the number thirty. As the lift moves, he closes his eyes again, hearing the distant alarm of a heart monitor and shouting, only to have the noise interrupted by the elevator's ding and the sound of the doors opening slowly.

"Breathe," he whispers to himself, entering the office full of people rushing to finish their articles. Dominic can't help but chuckle as he walks to the kitchen area, hearing a foot tapping behind him.

"You're late," Colin says, doing his best impression of Ashley. "So, what excuse is it this time?" he asks. Dominic looks over at Colin, who smiles at him. Dominic rolls his eyes as he hands Colin his tea. Colin accepts it whole heartedly. "Ooh, don't mind if I do." His hand reaches for the pastry bag but Dominic slaps it away.

"It's not for you," Dominic says, recycling the cup holder. Colin rubs his sore hand and Dominic laughs. As they make their way to Ashley's office, Dominic knocks on the door and walks in without waiting for an answer.

"I didn't realise we can pick and choose when we work. You're an hour late, Mr Wolf! That's a month you can deal with the printers," she snaps, not looking up from her desk as she sorts through several documents.

"I'm sorry, I was catching up with Mr and Mrs M," Dominic says as he hands the pastry bag over. Ashley looks up at him and her face falls.

"Levi's anniversary. Can't believe it's already that time of year. I should visit his parents soon," she whispers. Colin leans against a nearby table. Next to him is a picture of Ashley, Colin, Levi and Dominic; their smiles beaming are still contagious even through the picture frame. The red and blue plaid shirt he wears in the picture was one of his favourites. His bad habit of leaving his glasses in his belt is visible as he holds a beer in one hand with his arm wrapped around Dominic's waist.

"Levi was one of the best photographers and bakers," Colin says, looking over to Dominic. "And one of my best friends."

Ashley looks at them both and a sweet, sad smile tugs at her lips. She turns to the photo. "He was, wasn't he?"

Dominic chokes. "He was my one and only." Colin places his hand on Dominic's shoulder to comfort him as the room falls silent.

Clearing his throat, Dominic begins to speak. "Ashley, about the article I was writing about the current events—"

"Binned," says Ashley, interrupting Dominic as she rips the pastry bag open to reveal the delicious Danish. "I want you to do something completely different." She starts eating the pastry. Colin sips his tea as he watches the exchange between the two of them.

"Like what?" Dominic questions, clearly irritated. Ashley looks at Colin then back to Dominic. Leaving her chair, she shows Dominic his previous articles. "You want me to do an article on this?" he asks in confusion.

Ashley sighs in irritation, "No, you idiot. I want you to write an article with a light-hearted theme; something you used to do. Like these," she says, kindly tapping on the articles in front of her. "You did such wonderful articles that drew readers in, not tear them apart. The amount of angry mail that comes in now is ridiculous." Colin walks over and pats Dominic on the shoulder. "Do an article on love," he suggests. Ashley glares at him, but after a few seconds of debating in her head she nods in agreement, handing Dominic a folder.

"Colin volunteers at a retirement home every now and then just outside the city. Go with him." Dominic opens the folders to look at pictures of Colin volunteering and the notes on different occupants. "Now that I've said my piece and you've bribed me with the goods, get out!" she says, sending them a teasing smile.

Colin and Dominic make their way out of her office. "Love…" Dominic whispers, looking at Colin who is smiling a little.

"You have to start talking about Levi and the love you had for him, and soon," Colin says, giving him a look as he raises his cup. "As always, thank you for the tea." They go to their desks.

Dominic's desk is piled high with paper and packages. He pushes them aside so he can get to his laptop buried beneath it all. Sitting in his chair, Dominic moves to one side of his desk, and then swings back to the other. His eyes fall on a picture of himself and Levi outside the entrance of a circus.

Dominic smiles as he recalls the memory of himself and Levi at the circus. His smile grows as it was filled with many emotions, Dominic's surprise was almost caught by Levi so he sprung is proposal quicker than he expected. It was that day they decided to adopt, the day they spoke about their life together. Levi was special to Dominic in so many ways. They grew up together as best friends which gave them such a strong bond. When Dominic came out to his parents, Levi supported him whilst waiting to take his hand and claim him as his own. It didn't take long, in school they were never apart. Isaac, whose Dominics brother in law now, supported their relationship through school. When college came, both knew what they wanted to do. Levi was already a young celebrated photographer and a genius. He wanted to travel the world and take photographs and Dominic wanted to be a journalist.

They went to the same college and met Colin at. They all got along well and supported each other, but as the courses progressed they became stressful and the relationship suffered.

16

Dominic and Levi began to drift apart, they both knew it. Levi was scared; they were going to break up. Dominic felt the same but also knew that is not what he wanted and thought that Levi felt the same way. They sat down together one evening and talked about their insecurity's and what they wanted. Which was each other.

After that talk things were resolved. The three friends all got into the same university where they met Ashley, and, of course, Colin became smitten with her.

Their dream jobs became a reality. Soon after their second year of university, their talents were spotted and life started to work out for them. Ashley, Colin and Levi all worked together, Levi as a freelance photographer, Colin and Dominic as journalists at Ashley's father's very own newspaper. Isaac had become a barber and loved every second of it and married Dominic's sister. Dominic and Levi got married and for five were the best anyone could have asked for.

Levi was driving home one day after he collected a surprise for Dominic. It was a photo collage of all their times together over the years and included news of their success in their application to adopt a child. Then, a lorry driver texting on his phone suddenly lost control of his vehicle and collided with a wall, hitting Levi and several pedestrians in the process. The scene was horrific. The lorry driver was convicted for reckless driving and manslaughter, was banned from driving, and was sent to prison for fifteen years.

Levi died after arriving at the hospital. Dominic was given Levi's blood-stained belongings, amongst which was his collage, covered in his blood. The lift broke down in the hospital, leaving Dominic trapped with Levi's blood-stained items.

Dominic has suffered with panic attacks ever since, finding

small spaces, lifts, and cars the most difficult to deal with. After the accident, life has been hard for Dominic.

Stroking the picture, Dominic smiles. "Well, I better start writing then. Right, Levi?" Dominic asks, touching the photo slightly as he places it carefully on his desk. As his screen switches on, the document loads up with its dreaded blank page. Dominic drinks some of his vanilla coffee and sighs, his fingertips hesitantly hovering over the keyboard.

Dominic begins to type, pressing one key after the other into place, quickening as he finds his rhythm. It's as if the keys are possessed.

Do you believe in love? Have you ever been in love? Where you felt your heartbeat quicken at the slightest touch? Where you stomach is filled with butterflies? Do you remember that moment?

The moment the first kiss sparks everything; the way your loved one moves, smells, smiles, listens, and laughs with you? That one moment you knew that they were the one for you? I do. It is the best feeling in the world; everything is brighter, you feel so much better in yourself. As if the world could not defeat you if it went against you.

Do you believe you have a soul mate? What about a fated one? Or cupid's arrow? Or even the red string? There are so many stories that talk about love, where each person finds their love and did what they could to make it happen, to keep the bond between each other. Even in films you can tell how it ends. Can we make it happen, not in the way of movies, but by meeting someone and having that connection or spark and thinking they're the one? Is that even possible? What about the taste of victory when they accept your love and all the faults you have and the quirks that make you, you?

This article was assigned to me because of something I once was able to do. So, here it is. The article on love, and the one moment when we know it is meant to be.

Dominic leans back in his chair as he looks at his work. He has made a start; now he just needs a story. But who? Who would give him a story?

Colin taps him on the shoulder. "You ready for lunch?" he asks. Dominic looks over at the clock on the wall, ticking away happily.

"Yeah. Hey, when do you go to that nursing home?"

Colin looks at him and shrugs. "When I can, really." Dominic nods. "In a couple of weeks I'm volunteering there, did you want to join me?" Colin asks, as they walk side by side towards the kitchen.

Suddenly, someone bumps into Dominic in the kitchen, spilling water everywhere. "No, no, oh my God—I'm so sorry," Blake stutters as he begins to freak out, grabbing a bunch of nearby napkins to clean up the mess spilling on the floor.

"Hey, it's fine. It's only water," Dominic says, looking at the panicking man.

Blake has short brown hair and wears a shirt tucked into his trousers and shiny shoes. He looks as if he is in his late twenties.

"Are you new here?" Colin asks, helping pick up the items that fell during the spectacular event while Dominic pours him a new drink.

Blake looks at him and smiles. "Yeah, how did you know?" he asks with enthusiasm in his voice.

Dominic chuckles a little. "Colin is good at reading people." He smiles as he offers the young man a bag and his cup.

"What's this?" he asks, taking it hesitantly from him. Dominic sighs as he looks to Colin who continues for him.

19

"So, are you an intern or here for work experience?" Colin asks the young man, who shakes his head while smiling in slight embarrassment

"I work here. Seems my baby face has done it again."

Colin nods his head slowly. "Ha-ha, sorry about that. Dominic's given it to you as an apology. You see, he's not really good at voicing them." Blake's brown eyes widen as he turns to look at Dominic.

"You're Dominic Wolf?" he cries loudly. Colin looks at him, trying hard to suppress his laughter. "The Dominic Wolf!"

Dominic looks over to Colin who nudges him. "What's your name?" Dominic asks.

"My name? My name is Blake. Blake Evans."

Dominic nods. "Enjoy your lunch," he says, leaving the kitchen with a banana, apple, and orange. Colin follows behind him, waving at Blake who now has a slight blush on his face.

"Blake, huh?" Colin whispers.

"Shut up." Dominic hushes him while Colin laughs like a boy teasing his friend over a crush as they both head towards the rooftop.

The rooftop has been decorated to help de-stress the employees. Plants and pictures are displayed everywhere. Each seating area has a covering to protect people from the wind and rain and has wooden beams covered in plants that intertwine in holes with flowers that bloom over the seasons. There are benches for smokers and non-smokers kept at distance, so no one would suffer from second-hand smoke or complain about the smell. Two entrances to the roof were made so all staff can happily access the roof without going through the smoker's area. There are also small tables where employees can eat their lunch and drink while reading magazines during their breaks, if they wish to do so. The rooftop is thought out well.

"So, are you going to come with me?" Colin asks, looking at Dominic. Dominic rubs his spiky chin. "Clean yourself up a bit if you are. When was the last time you saw a barber? Or a bath?" Colin scolds Dominic as they lean against the rails on the roof that looks over the city. The view from there is incredible; this is where they come to clear their heads and chat when they can.

"It's been a while," Dominic confesses with a heavy sigh.

"If you sigh one more time," Colin growls, looking at him from the corner of his eye. He takes a deep breath of the cool air around him and grabs a pack of cigarettes from his pocket, picking one that he'd prepared earlier.

"I thought you'd quit?" Dominic asks raising one eyebrow, questioning Colin.

Colin lights the cigarette, "I did…" he replies, watching the smoke leave the burning roll. "We're trying for a baby," Colin finally says out loud. Dominic has a smile on his face as he listens carefully to Colin. "Ashley's been so stressed lately that we haven't had time for ourselves. She's had other editors on her back and making her like…" He starts to trail off when he sees Dominic's grin. "What? I'm being serious here!" Colin exclaims, taking a deep breath of his cigarette when he chokes on it. He shakes his head, stubbing the cigarette and placing it back inside the box.

Dominic lifts his hands in the air and smiles. "No, I was just smiling. It's nice to hear you talk about her, about you guys. I remember you being the gentleman player." He chuckles at the memory, giving Colin a gentle push causing him to laugh with Dominic.

"Yeah. I was, but Ashley is my one and only, you know." Colin sighs, looking away from Dominic as a smile crawls its way on to his face. "I love everything about her. I can't believe we've been married for eight years." Dominic smiles at his friend and, patting his back, nods in silence.

"So, what do you think of the Blake kiddie?" Colin suddenly asks.

Dominic looks at him with an eyebrow raised. "Ah, remember – he's not a kiddie. What about him?" he asks, slightly annoyed. Colin laughs at his friend's reaction, unaware that Blake is by the door listening to their conversation.

"Come on, he was all gooey eyes at you." Colin leans against Dominic as he rubs the back of his neck.

"He's a good kid and I don't think it's a good idea for him to get involved with me." As Dominic speaks, each word is tinged with a slight sadness. Colin moves away from him, staring at him with sad eyes.

"Levi would want you to be happy, not moping about, Dom. You have to remember the happy memories and share them with a new love." Colin sighs, looking for his gum to chew. With no luck, he tuts in annoyance. "It doesn't have to be Blake, but you have to move on at your own pace. Levi wouldn't want you to be sad all the time," Colin reminds him as he puts his cigarette box in a nearby bin.

"Colin…" Dominic starts.

Colin grins. "Never mind."

Blake returns inside after listening to the conversation. "Blake, right? Get me a coffee, won't you?" Mr Sims demands as he shoves his cup into Blake's hand.

Blake just smiles and nods, disappearing into the kitchen. His thoughts drift back to the conversation he heard. "Levi?" he whispers thoughtfully, the name sounding familiar.

Ashley walks into the kitchen and sees Blake. "Ah, Blake

right – the new guy?" Blake nods. Ashley smiles sweetly at him. "Having a coffee?" she asks, holding up the coffee pot.

Blake nods. "Thank you. Mr Sims always has a black coffee," he replies as he places two teaspoons full of coffee in the cup. Ashley looks at him and then to Mr Sims' desk, where he sits laughing with other employees

"Blake, I'll take it over to him. But first, a little advice. Don't let people walk over you in this business. Especially if you think you're being nice," she says, smiling as she finishes making the coffee.

Blake nods, watching Ashley take the cup and place it on Mr Sims' table. Spinning in his chair, his face pales. "Ashley, I— uh—" he starts panicking, as do the other employees as they scurry to their desks. She leans down to whisper something into his ear and he pales even more, if that was humanly possible. Dominic and Colin return from their break. "Ashley strikes again!" Dominic says, laughing slightly.

Colin looks to Blake and smiles. "Let me guess. Sim's asked you to do his coffee, his paperwork, and photocopying because you'd be doing him a massive favour?"

Blake nods in confusion. "Yeah, how did you know?"

Dominic shakes his head. "Blake, Sims is known as a class A dirt bag. Just steer clear and you'll be fine," he says, patting Blake on the back.

"Right, I'm off. I have to do some recon on love," Dominic says, using finger quotes as he says the word love. Blake watches him head to the lift.

"Aren't you going with him?" Colin asks. "He might get snatched by someone if you stay here." Blake looks to Colin for a second before chasing after Dominic.

"Wait, Mr Wolf!" Blake shouts as he grabs his jacket and

camera.

"You are an evil man, Colin." Ashley chuckles as she stands next to him, watching the sight of Blake leaving with Dominic.

"He reminds me a little of Levi when we first met him in college. That fresh look..." Colin says with a slight chuckle. Ashley nods her head in agreement before she looks at him.

"You have work to do," she reminds him.

"Yes, boss." A cheeky smile spreads across his face.

Chapter 2

Surrounded by lush green grass and swaying trees, Blake sits on a bench made of swirl-patterned steel watching Dominic. In his lap is a small package in a paper bag. Dominic is taking notes and pictures of the area and of the people walking or sitting in the park.

"Mr Wolf, don't you think you should take a break?" he calls to him, but Dominic can't hear him. Seeing a ball that had strayed, Blake kicks it hard enough to give it height and watches it collide with the back of Dominic's head. Stifling a laugh, Blake watches a nearby man wince. Kids who are watching burst into laughter, and seeing this, Blake takes the chance to capture a picture of them all in a group, some bent over holding their stomachs. Dominic kicks the ball to them, rubbing his head as he watches them return to their game of football.

"That's a good picture," Dominic praises, looking over Blake's shoulder and making him jump. Blake looks up to find Dominic is closer. Dominic, still looking at the camera, takes it away from his hands and flips through the photos. Blake tries to make a grab for it but Dominic, being childish, moves it away every time he jumps for it.

"Please give it back! It's expensive," Blake pleads. Dominic smiles as he looks through the pictures and stops when one catches his eye.

Blake uses this chance to snatch it out of his hands.

"Those pictures, when did you take them?" Dominic asks,

almost in a whisper. Blake looks at the screen. There in the camera are pictures of Dominic and Levi when Dominic proposed. One picture shows Levi jumping into Dominic's arms where the two form a massive hug. Dominic's grin is huge.

"Ah those two. They're good, aren't they? You can tell that he's so happy. The man who proposed really loves him," Blake says with a warm smile. "I like these photos because you can feel the love and warmth from them. I used these photos when I was in my final year of college. I won a competition with them."

Dominic stares at the picture of Levi in his arms. Blake looks towards him, noticing that Dominic is staring at the picture with so much longing and heartache that tears slowly start to form.

"These are the only pictures I couldn't find," Dominic says in between silent sobs. "And to think that they were with you the whole time," he says, laughing. Dominic looks to Blake with a smile – a real smile. "Would it be possible to have these to give to his mum?" Dominic asks. Blake blinks before giving a nod in confusion. Blake hands the camera back to Dominic so he can have another look, Dominic flicks between the pictures on the camera with a gentle smile.

"Not for yourself?" Blake thinks as he continues to watch Dominic.

Dominic looks to Blake and suddenly nods as if confirming a plan within his head. "Blake, you're going to help me with the article, right?" he asks, wiping his tears off his face.

Blake straightens himself up. "Yes, I will, as much as possible." Dominic smiles, wrapping his arm around his shoulder.

"Good. In that case I know where we can go to think of a plan," Dominic says, chuckling.

In the office, Ashley has finally finished looking over the

documents on her desk when she receives a phone call. "Yes, Ashley here." The other end of the phone is a voice she knows all too well, and she can't help but smile.

"Yes, hello. It's Colin. I was wondering if it was possible for me to arrange a dinner for just the two of us at a little Italian place I know," Colin says as he continues to type on his computer.

Ashley swings her chair around to face the view of the city. "Well, that is certainly tempting, but what's the occasion?" she asks, slightly amused.

"I love you," Colin says meaningfully.

Ashley's breathing hitches a little. Oh, this man knows how to wrap her around his finger. "I love you, too. Yes, that would be nice."

Colin chuckles at the response on the phone. "See you tonight then." With that, the phone clicks off.

Colin rises from his chair, making his way to her office. With a slight tap he enters before she answers the door.

"Paperwork is ready. I'm going to head out of the office for an hour," Colin says coolly. Ashley nods her head.

When Colin leaves, he runs out the office, tripping slightly as he goes. Ashley watches and laughs, shaking her head before picking up the paperwork he left behind.

After a ten-minute bus ride, Colin arrives at a doctor's surgery. The clean, white walls surround him with posters of the flu and diabetes dotted around the waiting room. His leg bounces in an impatient manner when he's eventually called.

The doctor is tall and lanky and his glasses are round and sit at the end of his nose. "According to your notes, the first sample we took, result came back as insufficient tissue," the doctor says, looking at the computer screen. "With the new test results back, they appear normal. Which is great news."

27

Colin breathes a sigh of relief.

"So, you should be able to have children, but please remember there are other factors that can occur that may cause an inability to conceive, such as stress in your environment, obesity, and drug abuse. But, as there as there is no problem with obesity or drug abuse, I must ask if there is stress in your environment of work or home?"

Colin laughs slightly without meaning to, causing the doctor to raise his eyebrow out of irritation.

"You need to take this seriously, Colin, and please don't forget this also applies to your partner," the doctor says.

"I am. It's just that trying to get away from stress in the job that I do – that my wife and I do – is impossible." Colin leans into his chair, sighing as he looks seriously at the doctor. The doctor sighs with him. Colin leans forward in his chair.

"We both want kids. I want kids, she wants kids, but we're both…" His sentence starts to trail off. "My wife is an amazing woman, Doctor, and I am willing to do anything – and I mean anything – to get what she wants, and what we want."

The Doctor smiles and nods. "Well, as long as you stay healthy and avoid stress, there should be no problems. She must be one lucky woman."

Colin shakes his head and smiles at the Doctors comment. "No. I'm one lucky man." With a smile that says it all, Colin stands up and shakes the hand of the doctor, glad to have received the news he has so desperately been waiting to hear.

All of a sudden, Colin's phone rings. He sees it's Ashley and picks up. "Hey, honey, I was just on my way back. I've made the reservation and I have something to tell you," Colin says, before Ashley has a chance to say anything.

Ashley smiles. "Perfect. I'll see you in a couple of hours."

After some hours, Ashley finally leaves the office, saying goodbye to the security guard. Colin had left an hour before her, so she looks forward to seeing him. Getting in a taxi, Ashley heads to the Italian restaurant: the one with the cheesy garlic bread, so famous that in order to get a table there is a six month wait.

"I have a table with—" she begins.

"Ashley!" Colin calls to her with a grin on his face. The waitress smiles and shows Ashley to the table and she throws her arms around Colin's neck.

"Colin, it was such a long day." She sighs into his neck, breathing in his cologne. He gently squeezes her.

"Mmm, it's good to have time to ourselves," Colin whispers happily, kissing her cheek, then her forehead, and finally her lips. "Cherry?"

Ashley gently taps his arm, laughing at his comment as they sit at their table.

"I've got the white wine coming, but I didn't know if you want the usual or something different?" Colin says with a smile, "I've got the white win coming, but I didn't know if you want the usual or something different? And I ordered your favourite meal."

Ashley shakes her head. "The usual is perfect." He smiles and nods to the waiter who heads to the kitchen. Moments later white wine was brought to their table. Colin nodded at the bottle, the waiter poured each of the them a glass and placed the bottle on the table before leaving them once more.

"So, what did you want to talk about?" Ashley asks as she sips the wine.

"I was given the all clear," Colin says excitedly with a grin. Ashley blinks a few times as she processes the news. A smile spreads on her face and happy tears start to spill out. She leaps out of her chair and hugs Colin who hastily rises from his chair.

"Really?" she asks in disbelief. He nods as he chokes back tears of his own.

"And I was thinking that I could be a stay-at-home, Dad, so you can carry on doing what you love without worrying about work or our child," Colin says whilst squeezing Ashley, as happy as he thinks he can be.

Ashley nods into his neck as happy tears continue to fall. "Let's think of that when we get there," she says.

"Your food is ready," a waiter says, feeling a little awkward. Standing with him is an older gentleman.

"Dad?" Colin exclaims, surprised.

"Congratulations, Ashley and Colin. I'm so pleased for you." In his hand is a bouquet of flowers.

Colin looks to Matthias even though he told his dad about what was happening; he didn't expect him to appear tonight. "Thank you, Dad." Colin smiles at his father. Ashley lets go of Colin, grinning through the tears and accepts the flowers from Colin's dad, thanking him with a kiss to the cheeks.

"Thank you, Mr Moretti," Ashley says.

Matthias smiles as he looks at them both with a grin. "Please, call me Matthias. My family… such a beautiful family. Remember, we're here for you no matter what." With that, he leaves them to eat their food and enjoy each other's company.
The night is happy and cheerful as they chat about names and memories. Matthias continues to see to other customers as it is rare for him to visit his restaurants. As the night continues, Ashley and Colin leave to head home.

A detached chocolate box cottage, on the outskirts of a London, a little home with black, wooden beams around the door and windows. The raw iron gate has pink roses decorating the edges and a lamp that sits at the top of the arch. Colin helps Ashley through the gate, and as they pass the flower filled garden, the scent is welcoming after the hard day and fun evening.

As they unlock the door they are greeted by a tabby cat and a German Shepherd. Colin laughs as the dog, Ollie, welcomes Ashley and the cat, Jazz, welcomes Colin.

"Kids, settle down, settle down," he laughs, picking up Jazz as she nuzzles her face into him.

"I'll see you in bed," Ashley says with a smile. Colin watches as she makes her way upstairs. He quickly takes his coat off as the tabby cat jumps out of his arms.

"Sorry, Jazz," he apologises. Kicking his shoes off by the shoe rack that sits by the door, Colin gives both pets their meals and treats and makes sure they settle into their beds in the living room.

Colin runs upstairs unbuttoning his shirt, carefully opening the bedroom door with one hand, only to find Ashley out for the count. A smile grows on Colin's face as he walks to Ashley's side of the bed. Gently sitting by her, he moves a stray strand of hair. "Hah, night Ash," he whispers, giving a gentle kiss on her forehead.

Carefully, he rises from the bed to get into his pyjamas that lay on his pillow. Finally, getting into bed, he smiles to himself. He can't help but feel like the happiest man in the world.

The next morning, they awake with the alarm demanding their attention. Ashley looks to Colin apologetically. "I'm sorry, I fell asleep first," she says, looking guilty.

Colin laughs, kissing her on cheek. "It's all right, you drank too much, so I wouldn't have done anything anyway except kiss and cuddle." Ashley blinks at him with a suspicious look.

Colin laughs. "What?"

"I would have attacked you," Ashley says, laughing. Colin imagines this for a moment before nodding and continuing to laugh with her.

Suddenly, Colin is pushed down into the bed, her bed hair blocking his view. "We're going to be late you know," he reminds Ashley, teasing her slightly. He places some of her hair behind her ear and she smiles, kissing his hand.

"It'll be fine. You have to go to the home today, and I already said I won't be in until the afternoon," Ashley whispers, kissing his lips.

Colin laughs. "If the boss says so." Ashley chuckles as Colin switches their positions and they enjoy their morning together for the first time in a long time. He's off to the home and she's going in for the afternoon.

Chapter 3

"Mr Wolf," Blake calls to Dominic, panting. Dominic is sipping his morning coffee as usual at the café, and, hearing Blake, looks over to him. Blake is leaning on his knees trying to catch his breath. "I'm sorry. I'm late." Blake apologises between each deep breath.

Dominic laughs slightly as he speaks. "There's no need to apologise. Besides, you're not late. I was simply early," he says, sliding a cup towards him along with a plate with a blueberry muffin on it. "Sit down and catch your breath."

All of a sudden, Mrs M comes over with a bag. "Dom, why don't you eat something different for a change?" she questions him with a worried scowl. Placing the bag gently on the table, she looks towards Blake and a grin plays across her face. "Mr M, come and see this!" she shouts in delight. Dominic sighs as he takes a sip of his coffee. Blake has finally taken a seat when Mrs M grabs his hands, pulling him to his feet. "Aren't you a cutie! So, where did Dom find you?" she asks as she looks him up and down. "You do photography?" she asks as her brow rises looking to his camera bag. Blake opens his mouth to answer her question, only to be interrupted. "Well, don't just stand there. Here, sit down." She returns him back to his chair and Blake looks to Dominic for help, but he pays no attention as he continues to play innocent, drinking his coffee.

Mr M comes out of the kitchen to join them, looking at his wife with a tired expression. "Mrs M, please leave the poor boy alone." He looks to Dominic and then to Blake and grins. "What would you like to drink?" Mr M asks Blake. Blake can't keep up with them; the pair are like a whirlwind.

Dominic chuckles. "He'll have another cup of tea. This one has gone cold. Slightly strong, and a splash of milk with two sugars," Dominic says before taking a sip of his own coffee.

Blake looks to him surprised. "And I'll have a refill please, Mrs M." They both smile and Mrs M giggles.

As Mr and Mrs M disappear inside the café, Blake breathes a sigh of relief.

"What was all that about? You know how I like my tea?" Blake asks, mildly amused. Dominic smiles and shrugs, knowing full well what it was about and not answering his other question either. Dominic has watched him in the kitchen when he makes his tea.

Noting that Dominic is feigning any knowledge, Blake curiously asks, "So why are we meeting here so early?" He goes to peek in the bag that sits on the table, but Dominic skilfully moves it away. Doing so, a grin appears on his face when he spots a happy Ashley walking in their direction along with Colin, with grins on their faces from ear to ear.

"You'll see," is all he says.

"Thank you, Mr Wolf, as always," Ashley says, taking the bag from in front of him.

Instead of wearing his usual clean-cut suit, Colin is wearing grey joggers with cuffs at the bottom, black trainers, and a black t-shirt with a heartbeat in red. Colin smiles at Dominic who is wearing jeans and a t-shirt with a motorbike riding into the sunset. However, Dominic hasn't gone to the barber like he promised.

On the other hand, Blake is still wearing work clothes,

throwing Colin off completely. "I thought you were coming to the retirement home with us?" enquired Colin confused, as he pulls out a chair from the table.

Ashley stands behind him with her arms around his neck as she kisses his cheek. "I've got to go, see you later," she says, wiping her lipstick off his cheek.

With a smile, Colin gives her a peck in return. "Have a good day." He sends her off and watches her leave.

"Wait, what just happened?" Blake asks, utterly gobsmacked. Dominic and Colin ignore the question by the shocked Blake.

"You can't go looking like that," Colin says, gesturing to Dominic.

"Why, what's wrong with it?" Dominic asks.

"You look a mess," Mrs M interjects whilst coming out with all their drinks, causing Colin to laugh.

"How did you know I was coming?" Colin asks.

"Don't underestimate me. Just because I look old doesn't mean I've lost my touch," Mrs M says, smiling at him. Colin chuckles and kisses her on the cheek in thanks.

"Blake, why are you dressed like a funeral director?" Colin returns his attention to him as he takes a sip of his tea. As a satisfied sigh escapes Colin's lips he leans back into his chair, relaxing.

"I'm not dressed as a funeral director. These are my work clothes." Blake pouts, and as he looks down at his outfit a small frown etches on to his brow. Dominic looks at Colin and shakes his head. Colin shrugs, making an innocent face when Dominic sends him a glare. Colin raises his hands and thinks of something to say to make up for what he said.

"You look good at work, but you have to consider that when

we get to the retirement home they may think of it differently," Colin explains. Dominic nods his head in agreement, unaware that he was next in the firing line. "Unlike Dom here, who looks like he's just been released from prison." Colin smirks as he tilts his head to look at Dominic.

Blake laughs and Colin and Dominic look at him. Dominic smiles a little. "Oh come on, I look good," he says as he flexes his biceps. Colin rolls his eyes as he pinches his tummy.

"Uh huh, totally." Colin laughs. Dominic laughs with him as he pinches Colin's tummy back. Blake watches the exchange, and smiles.

"So, what do we do after this?" Blake asks as he finishes his tea. Colin hums at his question as he takes a sip of his drink. "Take the gorilla to a barber, then go to the shop and sort you out," Colin says, nodding his head to confirm what he has lined up.

Blake and Dominic look to each other; Colin has done nothing but grin and pick on them since his arrival at the café. Mr and Mrs M come outside to take away their cups. "Be good, boys," Mrs M calls to them, smiling whilst her hazel eyes glisten. "Including you, Mr Moretti." Mrs M nods to him, and his grin grows bigger, if that was possible.

"Let's go." Colin cheers as they leave and Blake takes his wallet out when Mr M shakes his head.

"No need, you're one of Dominic and Colin's friends." With that, he finishes tucking the chair into the table and returns inside.

Mrs M smiles to the confused Blake. "I'm sure with time, Dominic will explain." She gently turns him around and pushes him towards them.

Blake smiles with a spring in his step and runs to catch up. Dominic pulls him forward by the wrist, so that he is now walking side by side with them.

Colin looks at his watch. "Right, so *he* should be open about now." Dominic nods as they slowly arrive at the crossing, waiting for the little red man to go green. Blake watches no cars and notices how people on their phones aren't really looking where they are going as they step out into the road as they try to cross from one side to the other. A flurry of car horns ring out along with shouts from amongst the crowds of people.

Dominic shakes his head and Colin looks to the people beside him, some on their phones, others listening to the music. Colin can't help but smile. Blake looks to Dominic and Colin. "Aren't we going to cross? There's no traffic." Dominic stares at him then shakes his head as he patiently waits for the little red man to turn green. They can hear a child whining and moaning at her mum about crossing the road.

Dominic looks to her and chuckles. He slowly walks over and bends down to the child's height. The girl grips her mother's hand. "Hey there, kid, my name is Mr Wolf." Dominic introduces himself with a gentle smile and her mum smiles and nods her head in a small hello.

With a smile still on her face the mum introduces herself. "Hello Mr Wolf. I'm Anna."

Her daughter looks to her mum, then back at Dominic. "… My name is Charlie." She swings Anna's hand a little while looking at him.

Dominic nods his head, "Hello, Charlie."

"Mr Wolf, she wants to cross the road, but I keep telling her that we can't," Anna explains as she gently strokes her daughter's black and tightly curled hair.

"Well, Charlie, you can't cross until the little green man says it's okay to cross," Dominic tells Charlie with a gentle smile.

Blake watches with a smile when he looks at Colin who stands next to him. He notices that Colin, on the other hand, is watching with a sad smile.

"But, Why?" Charlie whines.

"Well, because the little red and green men are run by fairies that are watching us cross the road. They make sure it's safe for us to cross, but when we cross on a red man and there is a car coming and something bad happens, they cry," Dominic explains to her. Anna smiles as Dominic does.

Charlie thinks for a while. "I don't want the fairies to cry. What happens to the fairies when they cry?"

"Neither do I. I don't want the fairies to cry, they'll lose their magic." Dominic replies.

"No!" Charlie shouts loudly, causing other adults to listen in to their conversation. Dominic nods his head. Charlie looks to her mother to confirm this; Anna nods in agreement. "Then, I won't cross until the green man shows." Dominic smiles and nods his head. "Good." Dominic says.

Charlie's mother mouths a thank you, and Dominic nods in response as he returns to Blake and Colin.

Suddenly, Charlie, at the top of her voice, shouts at the adults who attempt to cross the road. "Wait until the red man is green! You'll make the fairies sad!" Colin's cheeks puff out, trying his best not to laugh at the adults who return to the pavement. No one dares move until the little green man lights up. As it does, everyone crosses. Charlie waves as Dominic gives her a thumbs up and they part ways.

"So, the barber." Dominic coughs. Blake looks at Colin who can't help but chuckle, when a massive laugh erupts from behind them. A thick Scottish accent cuts through the air.

"Well look who finally decides to appear." Colin grins as he turns around and his grin only widens at the sight of the man. He is about six foot tall, his thick, black hair has small streaks of silver, his nicely groomed beard shapes his face, and his eyes are a cross between grey and blue. His well-groomed appearance is well known in the area he lives in. He is slightly chubby but still has a fair bit of muscle on him; the black t-shirt he wears makes that very obvious. Most of the women drool at the sight of him, but, unluckily for them, he is already taken. This is Isaac.

"Heh, Isaac, the Silver Fox! I didn't think you'd be here," Dominic exclaims, giving him a massive hug which is gladly returned.

"Ah, who's the youngster?" Isaac, who Dominic nicknames as Silver Fox, looks to Blake with a smile.

"Ah, yes. Blake, this is Isaac Wren, the best barber ever." Dominic introduces them. Blake nods to Isaac, extending his hand. Isaac yanks Blake into a bear hug.

Colin laughs. "Don't kill him – he's got a baby face," he says, reminding everyone. Isaac laughs, putting him down.

Suddenly, three kids come running. "Uncle Dom!" one cries, jumping up at him. Dominic catches him, swinging him round in a hug.

"Wow, look at you, you've grown Eddy!" Dominic exclaims.

"Uncle Colin," Ella says, sucking her thumb and pulling on Colin's tracksuit bottom. Colin smiles. Picking her up, he kisses her cheek several times.

"Ella, you are getting prettier every time I see you." She giggles and pokes his nose.

"Your uncles have come to me for a trim," Isaac says, laughing. Blake looks to all of them.

"This is Ed." Dominic introduces him, making Ed jump in

his arms once again. "That's Ella, and behind Isaac is George." Blake gives a small wave to George who ducks behind Isaac's leg.

"You'll have to excuse George. He's a little shy," Isaac says, picking him up and kissing him on the cheek. George wraps his arms around his neck keeping his face out of sight. Blake watches as George buries his face in his dad's shoulder. Blake nods with an understanding smile. They start chatting away and begin to follow Isaac to the barbers' shop.

Walking for another five minutes they reach a little pocket of shops. As they enter the red door of the Silver Fox Barbers the little bell rings. They are welcomed by people dancing to the song 'Footloose' playing on the radio at full volume, with customers laughing and clapping as the barbers and the receptionist dance.

The kids begin to giggle as they rush to join in. Ella runs over to someone singing into a hairbrush, whose hair is cut nicely with a design on each side of his head. The man, James, gently takes her hand and spins her around and her pink butterfly dress lifts with the spin. Ed runs and slides on his knees to another barber who is doing some foot work, wearing a badge with the name Clive. Helping Ed up, they begin to move in sync with their foot work. George jumps down from Isaac and runs to Alice, the receptionist, to join in the fun.

Isaac crosses his arms, trying his best not to smile at the scene but he can't help it. The customers are used to the fun, chilled atmosphere and love every second; that is why they come back. Isaac soon joins in when he notices his wife has snuck in holding a mug. He slides over and catches her, spinning her around after skilfully placing her drink somewhere safe.

Blake, Dominic, and Colin can't help but tap their feet along with the music. When it's over, they all clap and wolf whistle and

Isaac playfully slaps the side of his barbers' heads.

"Get back to work!" Isaac laughs and kisses his wife's cheek.

"That's Sarah, Dom's sister. She's partially deaf – when you talk to her, make sure you're facing her," Colin whispers into Blake's ear. Blake nods when Sarah spots Dominic. She rolls up a newspaper and starts hitting him while telling him off.

"You look a mess! I can't believe this, look at you," she scolds.

While Colin and Isaac are laughing, Clive watches in the mirror. "Yeah, you tell him Sarah." He cheers Sarah on and James joins in with the laughter and cheers too. Alice can't help but smile with George sitting on her lap.

"Come on, Sarah, give me a break would ya! I mean—" Another smack comes down.

"I can't believe I have you as a brother," Sarah sighs, finally. She looks to Colin. Unfortunately for him, he is next in line for a beating. "And you!" she scowls, holding the rolled-up newspaper when her eyes fall on Blake who Colin hides behind.

"Blake Evans?" she asks, almost in shock. Blake blinks in confusion and tilts his head slightly. She runs out of the room. Crashing can be heard in the other room and Isaac stands there and when he looks at everyone for some sort of answer, they shrug. Sarah comes running back out with a photo book.

Blake looks at her and sucks in a gasp of air. "I love your photos," she says with a grin, "Especially this one." She opens the book to the photos that Dominic has recently become aware of.

"Did you know that these two are in fact—" Sarah is cut off by Dominic who calls to Isaac loudly.

"Isaac, could you do me a favour and clean me up?" he asks. Isaac laughs and nods his head.

Colin looks to Sarah and realises what she's about to say. "Never mind. I'll tell you another time, I'm sure." Closing the book, she smiles at him. Blake picks up a pen and signs the inside of the book.

Dear Sarah,

Thank you to my first fan – well, my official first fan. I look forward to meeting you more and I hope you enjoy more of my work.

Best wishes and with much love,

Blake Evans

Sarah smiles and kisses his cheek. Isaac signs and says to her from across the room, "I saw that!" She sticks her tongue out at him in response. Laughter soon fills the barber shop. Sarah disappears to the other room once again, returning the book to its safe spot.

When Sarah returns, she brings with her a change of clothes. Dominic knows where she got them from, and he doesn't say anything.

Colin is finally happy with the clean shaven and freshly cut Dominic Wolf.

"Look at you," Isaac says, laughing.

"It's a miracle!" Colin jokes.

"Right, let's go." Colin cheers as he waves to them all. Dominic kisses his sister on the cheek and waves goodbye to the others.

"Your uncles are always causing trouble. I've missed it," Isaac says to Ella and George, who giggle in response.

"Off to the nursing home," Colin chimes as he hums the tune from the Wizard of Oz.

Dominic strokes his chin. "My chin's cold."

Blake laughs as he looks to Dominic, and Colin shakes his

42

head whilst also laughing at Dominic's remark. Blake looks at his watch; it's twelve o'clock, just as Colin had said to him yesterday.

"So, how do we get there? Bus? Train?" Blake asks. Colin stops humming and looks back at him. Dominic is rummaging through his bag, making sure he has everything.

"Dominic is driving us there."

Blake looks at him in shock. "He can drive?"

Colin laughs at his comment. Dominic shakes his head as he chuckles to himself. "I may have given that impression, but I can definitely tell you I can drive. I also ride, and I have a licence to drive a minibus, a small lorry, and a tractor." Dominic speaks proudly, puffing his chest out slightly and causing them all to laugh.

"Here they are." Dominic pulls out his car keys. When they get to the car park, Colin starts walking to a classic car, its wine-red colour shining under the afternoon sun,

"This? We're going in this?" Blake looks at Dominic.

Dominic, shaking his head in disbelief at the comment made, opens the car door. "Just get your behind in the car."

Blake gets in. The seats are comfier than he was expecting. Colin watches as Dominic takes a few deep breaths before getting into the car. Colin's expression is a caring one and Blake watches Dominic as he slowly gets in, carefully closing the car door behind him. Dominic slowly wraps his fingers around the steering wheel when he feels a gentle warm hand touch his, one he has known before.

"It's okay," a voice he has heard many times over whispers.

Placing the keys in the ignition he starts the car up. "Ready?"

Chapter 4

The beautiful afternoon sun bounces off the lush green fields flashing by. Blake watches carefully, looking at the many colourful fields and the little country lanes that lead to small towns or farms where dry mud spreads over the road. The journey is smooth, which shows that the car has been kept in good condition.

"So, when we get to the nursing home in the town, we'll go to the reception and sign in as volunteers. We already have permission from the director of the company to ask questions, as long as we don't upset anyone there," Colin explains.

Dominic nods in agreement, his eyes focusing on the road as he concentrates on driving.

"Make sure you get permission to take photos," Colin reminds Blake.

After about an hour of driving they pull into a town. It's like stepping into a picture. They carry on driving past the town until they come across the signs to the retirement home. The home comes into view, with a lovely garden out front filled with all sorts of flowers. Petals fall in the wind, decorating the gates and the path that leads to the front door.

Blake is the first to get out of the car. Colin opens his door when he notices that Dominic hasn't let go of the steering wheel. Making his way round to Dominic's side, Colin sighs as he takes a deep breath. He opens the door and crouches slightly, leaning into the car.

"Hey, Dom. It's going to be okay. There's no pressure. We're all here safe and sound, thanks to you. Take as long as you need," Colin spoke softly, patting him on the arm. Colin smiles and moves away, walking to the boot. Waiting.

After a couple of minutes calming his heart, Dominic takes a deep breath. Letting go of the steering wheel, he gets out of the car and makes his way to the boot. Colin gives him a meaningful nod.

Dominic opens the boot to reveal its contents: a wicker basket. Pulling it out, the size becomes a little more monstrous. Colin helps by grabbing the other end, the crunching of the basket audible in his hands. They gently place it on the ground.

"You came prepared?" Colin laughs as he closes the boot door.

Dominic smiles. "Well, new people, boring routine. Why not give them a bit of fun?" Blake smiles at a new side of Dominic he is seeing. Blake has only read the dark and angry side of Dominic Wolf, one that left many people, politicians, companies, and industries quake at the mere mention of the name. Not many people know why he became like this, but those who did, say nothing of it.

Dominic looks to Blake. "Hey, stop daydreaming. Help me carry this in, please." He snaps Blake out of his thoughts, grabbing an end of the basket.

Walking into the reception area, the smell of lemongrass hits their noses. Dominic smiles as he sees an elderly woman pushing a zimmer frame into the living room.

"Afternoon, Mrs Mason," the receptionist calls to her.

"Eh? Afternoon? Oh, good. I haven't missed the pudding just yet then," the woman replies.

Blake smiles at the comment. He's glad the home doesn't

45

smell like a hospital; he always imagined it would.

"Mr Moretti, it's good to see you." The receptionist smiles. "We understand that you have brought your colleagues here but I need to run through some of the safety—"

Colin interrupts her. "The only person who will need to go through them will be Mr Evans," he says, placing his hands on Blake. The receptionist looks to Dominic, then at Colin. "I believe I have already sent the documentation regarding the matter." Colin speaks sternly but still keeps a business smile.

With a few clicks of the mouse and some clacks of the keyboard, the receptionist nods. "Yes, that's all fine. It's all there." Colin nods.

Into Colin's ear, Dominic whispers, "Nice to see you still have that talent, smooth talker."

Colin looks to Dominic using the same business smile. "I don't know what you mean."

Dominic laughs a little as he pats Blake's shoulder. "Good luck," Dominic whispers, a few seconds before Blake is whisked away. He's taken into the back room of the reception area and isn't seen for an hour.

Dominic and Colin enter the lounge room where some of the elderly residents are sat. Some are watching television or sitting in armchairs dozing in the afternoon sun, while others are playing cards, and a few are even on their own looking out the window.

Colin smiles when four old ladies cheer at the sight of him. They slowly get out of their seats, hobbling towards him almost like a flock of geese and Colin opens his arms out to greet them. Each of the ladies reach to give him a kiss on his cheek and gently squeeze his cheeks. "Good to see you, Colin," they chime in high spirits.

"It's good to see you all. Ms Pats, Miss Woods, Mrs Hunter

and Ms Snow." They all smile as Colin remembers each of their names.

"Oh, and who's this with you?" one of the ladies ask. Colin smiles as he turns to Dominic who put out his hand.

"My name is Dominic Wolf," he says. The ladies pull on his hand, dragging him into the middle of the room.

"So, you're Dominic Wolf?" they ask him. Dominic nods and looks over his shoulder to Colin who laughs a little as he watches the four women circle Dominic like sharks. Colin soon recovers from his laugh as he is tapped on the shoulder by another resident of the home, and begins to greet them and many others in the room.

"So, what brings you here?" Ms Pats asks. Ms Pats has curly white hair that sits perfectly on her head, almost like a cloud. Her blue eyes crinkle as she smiles and the soft smell of lavender coming from her makes Dominic smile and grow calmer.

"I'm here to get to know everyone. And if they'll allow me, I'd like to ask some questions and listen to their stories. Maybe even get some memorable pictures, like you lovely ladies."

Miss Woods chuckles at Dominic's answer. "Such a charmer. Honest answer, I don't think we'll mind." Miss Woods speaks with a hint of an Irish accent and Dominic nods as he looks to her. Her white hair has traces of brown and black at the roots and her hazel eyes shine as she laughs.

"Yes, but I'm also here to volunteer, so if you have anything you need please don't hesitate to ask," he adds with a gentle smile.

"How nice. So, how did you hear about this place then?" Mrs Hunter asks, her broad Welsh accent cutting through the air. Mrs Hunter has short white hair with interesting colours dotted through, and her perfume fills Dominic's nose, making it twitch slightly.

"I heard from Colin, but I already knew about this place." Dominic answers with a hint of sadness, causing the women to look at each other with curiosity.

"You did? Oh, I see. Is it your mother or father?" Ms Snow asks. Her white hair is fluffy – almost like sheep's wool but softer – and her glasses sit on the bridge of her nose, attached to a chain that dangles around her neck.

Dominic sighs a little. "It would have been for my mother. But she was too ill, so I sent her to a specialist home. Before that, I was looking after her. So, what have you ladies been up to until now?"

They all look to each other once again, then to Dominic. Grabbing his arms, they drag him to the table they were previously sitting at. Laughing, they pull him into the game and begin playing.

Blake soon comes into the room after being briefed on what to do if certain situations were to arise.

"Blake," Colin calls to him. "Stay with me. Let Dominic work his magic."

It isn't long before the basket's contents are emptied: board games and an old phonograph that has been modified slightly with some older hits that would have played while they were growing up. Some of the ladies are smiling and dancing; others share stories with about what they used to get up to. Blake and Colin have been making teas and coffees and supplying water for them, keeping an eye on things at the same time.

One man does not join in. Arnold sits by the window most days. As he flicks through photo albums, his expressions are always filled with love. Dominic notices an expression that he knows all too well. Arnold wears a navy-blue jumper with a plaid shirt peeking over the jumper's collar, accompanied with khaki shorts and odd socks in brown trainers.

"That's Arnold Lovelock," Ms Snow whispers by Dominic's side. "Miserable bugger," she adds. Dominic smiles at her and nods.

"Thank you." As Dominic says this, Dominic approaches Arnold as he'd been informed that Arnold is not the social type

Dominic sits opposite Arnold, staring out the window. Arnold is still looking at his album when he speaks. "I don't care who you are, or what you want. Buzz off!" Dominic doesn't say anything in response, nor does he move.

Arnold huffs and he doesn't press the matter when Dominic pulls out a pen and his pad, waiting silently when Arnold looks up at him. Arnold's hair is a mixture of white and black. His eyes narrow towards him, and as they do, they crinkle ever so slightly. When Dominic looks straight back at him, Arnold searches his deep blue eyes. As he does, he finds a similar feeling of loss and a new light rekindling.

Arnold shifts in his seat. "What's your name, son?"

"Dominic Wolf, sir." Dominic gives a small smile. "And yourself?" He offers his hand out and Arnold takes it, firmly giving it a short shake.

"Arnold Lovelock," he says. As they exchange the small greeting the awkward atmosphere evaporates. The ladies, Colin, and Blake are all watching and are left with mouths gaping at the unfamiliar scene. Well, Colin isn't as shocked; he's more impressed that Dominic still has it in him.

"Wow! the old grump has finally made a friend." Ms Pats speaks harshly with a slight snort. Ms Snow looks to her and then to Colin.

"I'm assuming this is one of your ideas to get that old coot to lighten up?" she asks with amusement. Colin holds his hands up when a nurse comes in and sees Arnold having a conversation without looking cross for once.

"Wow!" she says, shocked. Colin nods as does some of the other residents.

"So, Dominic, what brings you here?" Arnold asks as he looks back and forth from his album to Dominic. Closing the album, Arnold gently clasps his hands together on top of it.

"I'm—I'm looking for a story about love and doing volunteer work at the same time." Dominic speaks slowly and softly as his eyes watch an elderly couple kissing each other on the bench. Arnold watches him closely.

"Whose?" Arnold asks.

Dominic smiles, looking directly in Arnold's eyes. "If you'll let me, I'd like to do yours."

Arnold lets out a little laugh as he leans forward a little. "No."

"Please, Arnold?" Dominic asks nicely, his eyes never leaving Arnold's. He isn't trying to be pushy, but he isn't giving up, unlike many who have done before. Arnold is used to pushy people, but something about Dominic Wolf is different.

"What do you want to know?" Arnold asks as he raises an eyebrow and leans back in his chair.

"Where you're from, where you were brought up, memories that stuck with you, and love. The one moment that you knew that she or he was going to be the one." Arnold listens to him as he thinks carefully; it is a lot that Dominic is asking of him. Arnold stares at Dominic and a silence falls for a while as he makes his decision.

"Come back tomorrow. Bring decent tea and whiskey. Then, I'll chat with you." Dominic smiles and nods. "But, in exchange,

50

I'm interested in yours." Dominic freezes. Arnold chuckles when he sees the pale Dominic.

"That's my deal." With that, Arnold picks up his album and begins to leave the lounge where the others follow in the same direction for dinner.

"What did he say?" Colin asks Dominic. Blake watches everyone leave.

"I—I have to think about this," Dominic says, sounding unsure. Colin looks to Blake who shrugs, unsure of what is happening.

They begin to leave the home and the journey back isn't as pleasant as their journey there. The silence is suffocating. Blake can see Dominic's expression sink and rise in colour as if his world is crumbling and rising around him. Whatever it is Dominic has to face, Blake and Colin are determined to be there to give him the gentle push he needs.

After arriving back, Colin texts Isaac to meet in a local pub. When they get there, Isaac is waiting with a massive grin on his face.

"So, Arnold wants you to tell him your story in exchange for yours?" Isaac repeats the deal between Dominic and Arnold with a hearty laugh. "I like this Arnold Lovelock," Isaac announces. Blake sips his drink, the ice cubes knocking against each other in the glass. Colin smiles at Blake who doesn't understand what is going on. Dominic is silent as he stares at the bottom of his drink, as if the soft amber liquid has the answer to all his problems.

"What do you think, Blake?" Colin asks him, giving Blake the chance to join in. Blake is taken back with the sudden question.

"Yeah, Blake, what do you think?" Isaac asks, giving him a bit of encouragement. Blake swallows his drink hard as he

51

glances to Dominic out of the corner of his eye.

"I—I think you should swap. I mean, a story for a story. But, I find it odd that he's suggested this sort of an exchange," Blake says as he fiddles with his empty glass. The pub they are in is the peaceful type; enough space for elbow room, the atmosphere is pleasant instead of stuffy, and there's no banging music or obnoxious laughter from overly drunk people that can be found in most pubs.

Dominic sits opposite them, listening to what they're saying. Blake is watching the way he frowns every now and then as if having a mental debate.

"Dominic?" Blake calls to him, bringing him out of his thoughts.

"Yeah?" he responds, lifting his cider to his lips.

Colin gives a sad smile as he watches his best friend still trying to let go of the weight on his shoulders, "Why not tell him? It would do you good."

Dominic swallows the last of his drink, looking to them as he nods. "I'm going to head off."

Blake looks to Isaac and Colin. "Was it something I said?" he asks, worried, as he looks towards the door after it slams shut. Colin shakes his head.

"No, not you. Nor I, nor Isaac. Dom has his story, but his life is just waiting for the next chapter. He just needs a little push for it to happen," Colin says, reassuring Blake.

Isaac looks to Colin before cracking a smile after a moment of silence. "Get you, Mr Poet."

Colin chuckles at Isaac's comment when Isaac's phone buzzes on the table. "Oh, that's me. I better get back then – see you guys soon," Isaac announces. Colin and Blake wave to Isaac as he leaves.

"It's to do with Levi, isn't it?" Blake asks suddenly. Colin looks at him with a slight smile.

"You knew him?" Colin asks. As Blake nods at his question, he grabs his camera, flicking through some of his photos. Finding the one Dominic reacted to in the park, he asks, "This is them, isn't it?"

Colin looks at the photo in shock. "How did you…" He trails off. Colin smiles and sinks in his seat a little as he sees how happy they are. How happy Dominic is.

"It was during my final year in college. I took pictures for a competition and I saw Dominic proposing, but at the time I didn't know that it was Levi and him. Levi is well known in the photography business – we study some of his techniques," Blake says, smiling at the memory. Colin smiles with him.

"So, what do you plan to do?" Colin asks him.

Blake looks at Colin, slightly tilting his head in response.

"Well, you like Dominic. Don't you?" Colin asks as a mischievous smile creeps onto his lips. Blake goes red quicker than a well-cooked lobster as he slams his hands on Colin. "What!" Colin exclaims rather loudly, and as he does, a slight glare is sent his way from the bartender.

Colin removes his hands as he shushes him in a giggle. "Keep your cool. Well, either way, I hope I can count on you and Dominic for this article." Colin laughs before he stands up. Blake stands with him, nodding towards the bartender who smiles in return, and they leave the pub.

"Well, kid, see you tomorrow." Colin waves goodbye. Blake nods as he watches him leave.

"Do I like Dominic?" Blake mumbles as he smiles slightly to himself, before shaking his head.

Chapter 5

Colin is the first to arrive at the café, Mrs M smiles with her usual greeting. Taking his order, she returns to their kitchen.

Dominic soon arrives. "What?" he asks. Colin laughs, shaking his head. Dominic has arrived wearing jeans and a casual black top with a denim jacket in his hand. "What? Does it not look okay? I don't want to look like I can't look after myself." Colin bursts out laughing at his retort.

"You look fine, now sit down and drink your vanilla coffee." Mrs M rolls her eyes as she watches them sit and wait for their final partner to arrive.

"Mr Wolf! Mr Moretti!" Blake's voice can be heard over the foot traffic and horns of the rush in the morning.

"Do you think he'll ever call us by our names when we're working together?" Colin asks as he sips his tea, watching the funny scene unfolding. Dominic simply shrugs as he enjoys his coffee.

"I'm sorry I'm late. There was a cat and this butterfly," Blake huffs as he leans on his knees.

"I'm not sure whether to take you literally or metaphorically." Dominic laughs and Colin rolls his eyes when Blake hands Dominic two envelopes.

"What's this?" Dominic asks as he begins to open the one with his name on it. Blake just gives a small smile. Inside are the photos of Levi and Dominic.

Dominic pulls Blake into a hug and Blake can't help but

notice that Dominic is actually quite strong and smells like earl grey and sandalwood. Blake can't help but close his eyes as he enjoys the sudden closeness. Colin smiles and then coughs.

As they separate in an awkward fashion, Dominic asks, "Ah, then, this is for his mum?" Blake nods.

Mrs M appears with a tray of drinks and a bag for Ashley. Dominic smiles and gives the envelope to Mrs M. After he takes the tray from her, which surprises Blake slightly, she smiles.

"What's this?" she asks in her warm voice, wiping her hands on her flour covered apron.

When she pulls the photos out, she gasps and tears well up in her eyes, "Luke!" she calls inside the café. Mr M comes out with soap on his hands.

"What? I'm washing up and I know I didn't make a mistake with the orders this time." His words trail off as he looks at the photos in her hands. Mr M sits on a nearby chair drying his hands into the towel that sits on his shoulder. Looking at the pictures, tears spring to his eyes. "That's our boy." He smiles, stroking the happy Levi. Dominic watches on, trying not to cry as he sees them lean against each other looking at the photos together with such love. "Thank you, Dominic. I know you have been looking for them." Dominic raises his hands and shakes his head as he pushes Blake forward.

"I took the photos," Blake states, smiling at them.

Mrs M pulls him into a massive hug, and as she tightens her arms she whispers a thank you.

Blake smiles and hugs her back just as hard.

Ashley appears and sees Colin smiling at the group of smiling and crying people, sipping his tea.

"Good morning, Mr Moretti. I see you have already started working," Ashley chuckles as she watches the scene with him.

Colin shakes his head, denying any involvement in the crying.

Blake moves his head to see her and Mrs M slowly lets him go and kisses him on the cheek. Blake straightens his shirt out and Colin laughs and smiles as he places his cup on the table and picks up her bag.

"Oh yeah. Good morning, Mrs Moretti," he says, having forgotten to greet her. Ashley kisses him on the lips and then wipes any of her lip gloss that remains.

"Wait, they're married?" Blake says, looking to Dominic as the realisation hits him. Dominic nods as he smiles before noticing what the time is.

"Good thing you're not a detective. We have to get going – Colin, come on." Colin nods to Dominic as he watches Ashley leave. As they start heading off, Mrs and Mr M wave them goodbye.

Once again, Colin looks at the classic car that Dominic is driving to the home. "Seriously? I thought you were going to change the car you drive this time," Colin teases as he looks at the wine-red car. Blake laughs when Dominic playfully glares at Colin. "Don't hate the car. I mean, you're more than welcome to walk there, or even get a bus." Colin raises his hands and shakes his head furiously. Dominic opens the boot, and puts his denim jacket next to the basket that he put into the boot this morning. After he shut the boot he walked around to the driver's side and looked to Colin.

"No, I love this car. I was joking!"

The journey is full of Colin's bad singing. Blake joins in on a couple of songs and the day is dry and cloudless with blue skies. Blake sighs as he watches the fields with tractors hard at work. "Would you ever live in the countryside?" Blake asks Colin and Dominic.

Dominic looks in the rear-view mirror. "I used to live in the countryside. I wouldn't mind moving back though. I have thought about it, but I would miss my friends too much." Colin laughs a little too.

"How about you, Mr Moretti?" Blake asks.

Colin turns around and looks him dead in the eye. "Stop calling me Mr Moretti. It's Colin, okay? We work together." Colin speaks sternly but his soft eyes make it feel like less of a telling off. Blake nods and Colin continues. "I'm the same. I would love to, but I would miss my friends. I have some family in the countryside," he adds.

Dominic comes to a stop. "Right, we have arrived," he says. Blake looks out and sees that it's busier than normal.

"What's going on?" he asks Dominic who lifts his nose to the air, the smell of cooked meats mixed with other scents making him sneeze a bit.

"Farmers' market." Dominic nods in confirmation.

Colin calls back to them both. "Oi! hurry up." Dominic runs over clutching his bag. Blake walks over to the home and he notices the name of the building is wrapped in ivy and white and royal purple weed flowers: Sunset Pearl Home. Blake takes a picture of it.

The women are stood in the doorway waiting for them to come in. "There you are!" They greet the boys in glee as Colin, Dominic, and Blake step into the living room. The others look on and greet them too. "It's good to see you," they say.

"I'm looking forward to the game again – I won't let you win this time," an elderly man says, smiling.

"I made some cakes with the help of the staff to keep us going," a lady next to him says, wearing a purple skirt. Her cling film skin tightens as she smiles and shows them the table they all excitedly put together.

"Did you bring that record I told you about?" Dominic smiles at the bustle that's begun. Colin pulls the basket in once again. The nurses are helping to set things up; they enjoy watching their residents laughing and smiling and they are glad because it has such an impact on their health.

Arnold is sitting in the corner staring out the window again. Dominic weaves through the elderly. "Arnold," Dominic calls to him, eventually reaching him. Gently seating himself in front of him, he asks, "Is it all right if I join you?" Arnold smiles and nods as he gestures at the seat in front of him.

"So, are you going to tell me your story?" Arnold asks, leaning back in his chair, Dominic slowly nods, ignoring his hands that are trembling ever so slightly.

"I'll make the tea first. The whiskey is a present." Dominic smiles as he hands over a tall round box. Arnold lets out a mighty laugh as he takes it, placing it by his chair.

"I was teasing about the whiskey, but I won't say no," he says.

Dominic returns with two cups of strong tea. "Hope this is okay." He places a little bowl of sugar taken from a nearby table. "Do you take sugar?" Dominic asks Arnold. Arnold shakes his head, taking a deep breath to the fresh tea made for him.

"Whenever you're ready then, Mr Wolf."

"His name was Levi. Levi Morstone." Dominic starts speaking as he looks out into the garden. He remembers it as clear as day, those memories he spent with Levi. And the moments he cherishes.

"I grew up with Levi. We were in the same neighbourhood and attended the same school. We were like two peas in a pod – we were inseparable. Levi had such an adventurous streak. Even when we were young, we got into all sorts of trouble. One time, we climbed the roof of my parents' kitchen so we could see the planes, another time we snuck out of class through the window, and there was also time when we were throwing fire work pellets.

"Levi always had a camera in his hands, sending pictures off to competitions. The pictures were either of nature, people, or landscapes. One of the pictures was of me in a puff of smoke. He won first place with that one. Levi would save any pocket money. When he did the paper round or when he won any competition, he put the money in a hidden pot under his bed so he could go to the college in the city to study photography without his parents having have to pay. You see Me and Levi went to school in the countryside, there wasn't a college or a university to help get to where wanted. We did whatever we could to do, to get out and make our dreams come to. For Levi it was those competitions and paper rounds. Levi's world was amazing, and I was a part of it. I never stopped loving him. I first realised when I was eleven. I tried hard not to, but I just couldn't help but love him.

"When we were sixteen, I came out to him, I hadn't had the courage to tell him that I loved him yet. It was the most nerve-racking thing I had ever done. You see, my parents loved me, and I loved them, but I didn't know how they would react when I would tell them that their son is gay.

"My sister always had her suspicions but I threw her off so she could never really say one hundred percent that I was gay. It was the first time Levi saw me cry, out of fear. But he took my hand in his and told me that 'No matter what life throws at us, we will always stick together. We are double the trouble and that is never going to change.'

"Levi hugged me until I stopped crying, but what we didn't

know was that his mum and dad were listening at the door. It was when I came downstairs that day to leave with him to tell my parents, that Mrs M, his mum, said to me, 'You'll always have a home here.'

When I got home with Levi, they were all there. My mum, dad, my older brother, and my sister. I took the biggest breath in and told them. The silence was horrible. It was like the whole world around me had stopped and started to close in on me. My mum smiled and told me, 'You're still my son and I don't care as long as you're happy, loved, healthy, and safe. That's all I want for you.' My dad, on the other hand, was quiet and left the room. I was a tiny bit shocked. We were always close, but it was difficult for him to digest. The next three days he didn't talk to me. He would go to say something and then walk the other way. Eventually, though, he came to my bedroom door and gave me a massive hug and told me, 'It doesn't change how much I love you. Just do me a favour – when you bring a boy round, introduce him with pride.' My older brother just shrugged. 'Does this mean I get his pudding tonight?' was all he asked. I don't think he really cared either way, which was so him. My sister just ran and hugged me. I think she knew all along.

"What I didn't expect was Levi to tell me that he liked me. 'I've always liked you, I thought it was just a brotherly love, but it's not,' he said. I pulled him into a hug, kissed him, and told him I felt the same way. I just wish I was the one who said it first.

"School was rough. Turned out someone found out that I was gay and dating Levi, so as you would expect, every now and then fights broke out between me and most of the boys in my year and older years. But, Isaac, who is now my sister's husband, was in the same year as me. Everyone steers clear of him – Isaac had a reputation for enjoying a fight and won all the time. What I didn't

60

know was at the time he was dating my sister Sarah. Out of the blue, he got involved in a fight and ever since then we were inseparable the three of us. And when we got into fights they weren't ever long. We rarely lost, thanks to Isaac. It's pretty much how I met him. Ever since then we fought together. But, no matter how hard I tried, Levi still managed to get bullied.

"Eventually, when we graduated, we left the countryside and moved to the city. I was studying journalism and he studied photography. We had a strong relationship, even when we weren't seeing each other very much because of distance or if work was our priority. When we did see each other, it was so precious time. Phones were off and we went out, sometimes we took off to somewhere quiet or stayed in and cooked together which we loved doing or if we were tired, ordered takeaway. I would work late with articles some nights with him, reading photo magazines, and he would work early and late with his photos sometimes, but we were together. So, when we had any fights, we tried to work things out as quickly as we could. When I missed him, I would cry some nights and then on his day off, we would take time off to make up for the time that made us feel lonely. We couldn't be without each other.

I had met Colin at college when I was studying journalism, later when we all went to the same university by some luck. We met Ashley. Ashley was on her way up in her job at The Astro and had her eye on Levi and I. She asked us how we would feel about working with her. I jumped at the chance but Levi took his time as he was still working on some jobs around the world.

"I started planning how I was going to ask him to marry me. I bought tickets to a circus that I knew was travelling to Europe soon, thanks to the journalism of course. I just needed to get money for an engagement ring.

"We finally moved in together when we finished university, and everything was so much better. He found out that his parents had opened a café in London and that it was running successfully thanks to Mrs M's cakes and amazing tea. The atmosphere she gives off is great, so he didn't have to worry about them.

"We both got our dream jobs in our own fields of work, and we were well known for it. Levi had a way with his photos that would pull you in to what he sees in the world and how he views everything. For example he would take a picture of an elderly couple for most people who'd view it, as just people waiting at bus stop sat on a bench in the cold as would I. Levi viewed it as an elderly couple in love and in their own world timeless and bound to each other.

"After a couple of years, of secretly dating Ashley and Colin announced their engagement, the two went to the registrar with myself and Levi as a witnesses and they had a wedding reception at Colin's fathers restaurant. It was quick and almost quiet. It wasn't long before my plans went into action. All the planning and all the saving I did has made it worth the wait. I can finally propose to Levi. I was terrified he would say no, but he didn't. He said yes, jumping into my arms. I didn't want to let go of him – not ever. I was finally going to spend the rest of my life with him. I was the happiest man in the world. I told him that when he first took my hand when I was sixteen he sealed my fate. As cheesy as it sounds, I guess I knew in that one moment, in that one small gesture, and loving thing he did. I knew we were meant to be.

The wedding was small-ish. His family, my family, our friends, and our colleagues celebrated our union. It was a day that we would never forget. Everyone we cared about was there. My mother and his mother had embarrassing photos everywhere at the reception, and my dad had a brilliant speech, telling stories of our childhood to make the room laugh. Then he made everyone cry by adding, 'Despite all the walls that they had to climb to get here, all those tears they've shed over the years, I have never seen two people that are made for each other more than Dominic and Levi. I wish them all the time that the world can give them, To their love, happiness and health'. My dad raised his glass to finish the toast. To their love and their health.' Isaac and Colin also made toast and speeches in the own way, in their own way.

"The party went on through the night until the morning of our honeymoon. We went travelling to all the places we wanted to go: Italy, Greece, Spain, Ireland, India, America, Nepal, Japan, Norway, Netherlands, back to Italy, and then eventually home. He took all the photos of course, and I was the pack horse. After a few years, we applied for adoption. We had been talking about it for a while. It was after Levi had been invited to several baby showers, we started to want our own family. After going through the interviews and red tape and waiting we finally heard from the adoption agency. Levi had told me that the letter from the agency came. He wanted to open it together, so he was on his way to see me after I had just finished an interview."

As Dominic stops talking his hands tighten in his lap. Arnold has been listening with a smile on his face up until now. Leaning back in his chair, Arnold places his head in his hand, waiting for Dominic's next words. Words that Arnold can probably guess.

Dominic takes a deep and shaky breath.

"I got a phone call from the hospital saying he was in an accident and to get to the hospital as soon as possible. I could feel my heart fall as I dropped the phone. Everything around me slowed as if time had stopped to be cruel for a few seconds to let the information sink in. I ran as fast as I could to the hospital. The interview was a few minutes away, but felt like it was miles away. As I was on the way, I saw what I assume was the crash site.

"The lorry was embedded in a wall of a building with several smashed cars dotted here and there. One of the cars I recognised. I shook my head. No. I didn't want to believe it. The debris was all over the place like the destruction left after a storm. I could feel my chest get tighter as I picked up my pace.

"I ran into the hospital shouting his name when a police officer gently grabbed me by the shoulder and asked if I was family. 'I'm his husband. Where is he? What happened? Is he okay? Please tell me he's okay?' I wasn't sure if it was my voice as I asked them all these questions, but they took me to where they had taken him.

"When I got there, it was like my chest had been kicked. Levi's brown, messy hair was covered in blood, his hands were badly scratched, and his clothes were covered in blood too. So much blood.

"Levi had an oxygen mask on when I noticed his eyes were looking at me. His muffled voice was calling my name. I tried to go to him but the police and hospital staff were holding me back all I could do was shout to him. I pushed and shoved my way through with all my strength as my fist punched one officer in the face, knocking him to the ground. Finally I was out of their hold and ran to Levi.

"Levi's breathing was shallow, his tears were falling down the edge of his eyes. There was just so much blood everywhere I looked. I could hear his heart monitor getting slower. He coughed and breathed hard as he lifted his hand. I grabbed it. 'Don't you dare leave me,' I begged.

"Levi gave a sad smile before squeezing his eyes shut and then open as more tears shed from both him and I. Levi choked, saying 'I love you.' I smiled through my tears, trying to get rid of them so I could see his face.

"'I love you too. So, so much.' I kissed his hands and then his face, stroking his hair. 'It's going to be okay. You hear me, Levi. You're going to be okay.' As I said this, he just smiled. His hand moved to my cheek his thumb, rubbing my tears away.

"'My big cry baby, I love you. Please be happy," he told me. As he closed his eyes I could feel the strength in his hand go. 'I love you.' He said it again. The doctor next to me looked at the monitor then started to address the nurses in the room as they moved around me. It wasn't long before they shoved me out of the way. I couldn't hear what was going on. It was like I was underwater.

"'Levi? Please don't leave me,' I whispered as the doctors pulled me away from him and handed me to the police officer I had punched. His firm grip held me in place before pulling me away. I felt so numb, like my body couldn't register what was happening. I was placed in the family waiting room when I could hear Mr M and Mrs M enter the room, calling my name.

"'Dominic, what's happening? Where's Levi?' I couldn't answer them and the police officer had to explain for me. Mrs M sat next to me on the sofa and held my hand tight as tears were running down my face. 'Dom,' she whispered.

"A doctor came in, their white coat flowing behind them. Again, I couldn't quite hear everything, but the one thing I remember hearing, and will remember for as long as I can, was 'I'm sorry, but Levi Wolf passed away.' Mrs M suddenly grabbed Mr M in a fit of tears and sobs. At that point the police officer left the room.

"Levi's heart had given out. He had massive blood loss, and there was no oxygen going to his brain... they did what they could but... they couldn't save him.

"I remember a nurse who handed me his things in a bag. Mr and Mrs M were waiting at our place. My place. Ashley, Colin, Sarah, and Isaac were going to be there for the news that he's gone. That he won't be coming back with me. I was at the lift waiting and I remember staring at my hands covered in his blood from where I was holding his hand and touching his head. Eventually, it arrived. Stepping in, the doors shut slowly and with a clunk I was leaving the building on my own. When the lift broke, I pressed all the buttons – even the bell button – for help, but nothing came. I looked at the bag the nurse gave me. Inside was Levi's photo collage and the letter from the adoption agency. It was a slap to the face. Everything was covered in crimson stains and the smell of blood flooded my nose. My breathing quickened as I remembered everything that had just happened. It was too much. Eventually, the lift started to work. I was a sweaty mess, short of breath, and sobbing.

"Since I was at an interview when I got the call, and my car was at the office I took a taxi home. I was in no fit state to drive. I didn't dare to look at Levi's things again.

"Mr and Mrs M were waiting at the our flat with the rest of the family. After arriving at our flat, Colin looked panicked as he looked behind me, Sarah was the same. Both looking for Levi.

"He's gone," was all I said, and the sobbing erupted in the room, Mr and Mrs M were holding each other, keening, crying and rocking. Ashley buried herself into Colin's chest as she sobbed, Colin's tears flowed down his face as he looked over to Isaac and nodded in my direction.

Isaac was already grabbing my arm and pulling me into a hug, it took me a single pat on the back before a sound erupted from me tears were just coming, it wasn't stopping, and every sound that came didn't sound like me. Sarah clung to me as she wrapped her arms from behind.

It was hours before they were ready to leave. Isaac were the last ones to leave. I had to push them out the door.

"As I grabbed one of his shirts and cradled it in my arms, my mum came in through the front door. I don't know why, but I still expected to see Levi come out from behind her, even though he wasn't going to. His laugh with his dimples showing, or his eyes lighting up when he knew his pranks and surprises worked. I wouldn't be able to see them anymore.

"'He's not going come home anymore. Is he?' Mum came to me, tearing up as she pulled me in, wrapping a blanket round us both. Levi's stuff was in the bag sitting by the mantelpiece. Mum gently pulled me to my feet and put me to bed.

"The collage was in a box tied up with a white and pink bow. With it was a white letter addressed to Mr L. and Mr D. Wolf that was smeared in blood. Levi's blood. Mum picked the bag up and started to place them in view for me to deal with in the morning.

"The next morning, I came down from my room to find my brother and my mum sitting at the kitchen table. My brother turned round and smiled. 'Morning,' he said. It was so carefree. He stood to pass me a coffee when I wrapped my arms around him. Laughing, he put the mug down and hugged me back.

"'What's in the letter?' he asked, being the nosey man that he is.

"'It's a letter to say whether or not we had been picked for adoption.' I didn't notice how small my voice was.

"'I know you're hurting right now. And what you need to do is cry, get angry, cry some more, drink a little, and then remember all the good things. All the amazing memories you have together,' he said. I nodded. That was the first time my brother had said something worth listening to, and I squeezed him and he squeezed me back before he returned to his normal painful self. After some time, they left. And I was alone in the empty house.

"Everything fell apart. I sobbed, clutching a pillow as I cried into it. I looked to the present and the letter. I took a deep breath and opened the box that was beautifully wrapped by Levi. I opened it to find pictures of us, our parents, Isaac and his family, Colin and Ashley, and more photos in a photo frame. In the corner was written, *Us and those we love, the treasures we share.* There was a sticky note on an empty spot, with the word *Proposal* on it. It was like a flood gate had opened. All I had building up was sadness, anger, and emptiness. There were things I had to make sure happened. My brother was right. But I jumped straight to anger instead.

"Revenge was something I didn't often take to in my line of work. But when I did. No one was safe. The man and the company he worked for had to pay, the other tabloids with their vulture like nature were sure to swoop in on this so they had to stay away so they couldn't interfere with it. As I made my way to leave the house, Colin was there. He came in and by the look on his face we had the same idea. It has been a couple of days since the accident and I needed this.

His plan was to leak the information to other tabloids about other stories worth their time so we could focus on this one. Colin was able to do that and we were able to uncover quite a bit as we worked together.

"Three weeks after, the man who had caused the incident had a court hearing, where a date would be set for the main hearing. It was set a month from that day. One of the best advantages of being friendly was that I had favours everywhere.

"However, before the date of the court hearing was

announced – so about two weeks after Levi's death – I paid a visit to the police station, where I met Officer Hugh who was at the scene and had held me back at the hospital. He was helping the detective. I had some questions I wanted to ask him, and wasn't leaving until I had answers. It took a lot of convincing for the officer to even let me hear anything about the investigation. However, I also said I was going to help.

"Giving them the name of an informant I use quite often, the police found all sorts of information that helped them with the investigation. Within a matter of days, they had CCTV footage and witness statements that would normally take weeks to collect. Documentation of the vehicle's MOT and then finding out that the driver who was being convicted had been warned, fined, given points on his licence, and had been banned from driving made the case impossible to lose. The police were thankful for the help provided by my informant, unaware that I was also going to destroy the company in the process. I had made my name: Dominic Wolf. The man that everyone knows today was born that day, fuelled by hatred, revenge, and anger. And I wasn't going to stop there.

"In a flash, the day of the funeral was here and I still hadn't opened the letter that sat on the mantelpiece at home. I was still scared to find out what lay written within the envelope.

"It was a lovely service from what I've been told. Truth be told I don't remember much. It was all a blur. People who worked with Levi from all over the world came to celebrate his life and to say their goodbyes. Mrs M was crying but smiling as people spoke to her about her son. Mr M was being hugged by everyone. I, on the other hand, was hiding. I couldn't face it, being told how sorry they were for my loss. I didn't want to be smothered. I had been doing that the past few weeks. In fact, I had been building up so much anger and hate for the outside world I was afraid it would explode. Isaac and Colin were close by to keep me in check.

While staring into the empty church I could hear the sound of a camera shutter. The sound of a photographer.

That was when I lost my cool. Everyone who was there saw a side of me I had kept hidden behind closed doors.

I found him, the nasty photographer hidden in the confession box. I pulled him by the scruff of the neck, dragging him out of the church. Around his neck was the camera, I ripped the camera from him. On the screen was Levi's coffin and me standing their touching where his head would be. When my thumb accidentally touched the screen it moved onto Mrs M crying into Mr M's chest and that's when I smashed the camera against the wall. I threw him on the floor along with his camera.

"All I wanted was privacy, but no! I couldn't get that. It's the funeral of my husband. Can you get that into your skull, hmm?" as I leaned over him, I grabbed his collar once again and gave him a quick punch in the face. Getting out of my grasp, the man scurried on his hands and knees as he tried to get some distance from me.

The man's lip bleeding from the punch I had given him. I remember Isaac standing behind me.

"I got hold of the man again. Isaac looked over his shoulder making sure the guests weren't following us." Mr M calmly lead everyone away saying that the uninvited guest was leaving.

Colin followed, as he watched me drag the photographer further away. I had moved the scene to around the back of the church away from prying eyes. Slamming him into the wall, I grabbed a fistful of his shirt, in a low growl I warned him, "if I see you, or anyone else-actually, no." I watched the photographers face pale when he realised I was no longer warning him. "Instead of just letting you off. Because lets face it you all do it. I'll crush the paper you work for and you will be the first to fall," Isaac pulled me away giving him the chance to run. As the man ran off, Colin watched him and a small grin claimed his face as he followed him.

"My hands were shaking so much. Isaac pulled me into a hug, and once again I held onto him, my hands shaking. Colin poked his head around the corner and Isaac looked over. Colin's hands were bruised and Isaac gave a small smile and rolled his eyes.

"Returning to the church, I had a bit more courage to say something to people who had come to say their goodbyes. I thanked them and sent them on their way. While we all knew Levi was the one who was good at that sort of thing." Levi was carefully placed into her ground and I was the last person left standing by his grave.

The priest was nice. He patted my back and told me 'They never truly leave, you know. The memories we have means they live on.' He led me out and I was able to leave.
"When I got home, I poured myself some whiskey. After a few seconds of sitting in silence I began to fulfil my promise.

"I pulled my laptop onto the table that sat in the middle of my living room and I called my informant like I had done many times before. 'Mark it's me… Yeah I need you to look someone up for me.' I was like a crazed animal, searching everything about the company, the Photographer had worked for. I found everything. All illegal activity they ever done, I found. Every ounce of evidence I compiled against them, I sent with the help of Mark to Officer Hugh in a gift envelope with the words *As a thank you* written on it. It was a couple weeks later that the

71

company was on the news and was closed down. CEO of the company was arrested for many offences, including illegal trespassing, wire-tapping, drug use, criminal damage, and blackmail.

"After I heard the news of the court case, I switched the telly off, and my eyes landed on the letter that still sat there, unopened. I took a gulp of liquid courage.

"Picking up the envelope that he had been protecting in the crash, it felt heavy in my hands. I ripped opened the letter. It sounded louder in the house on my own.

"As my eyes scanned the letter my eyes began to blur from the tears. I shouldn't have waited to read it. It was a letter from the adoption agency to say that they were congratulating us. We were getting a child. My heart was so heavy, I couldn't breathe properly, and my hands were shaking so much. I was sobbing uncontrollably, I had tried to phone but there weren't any words being formed. I sent a text instead to Colin and Isaac to meet me at the café the next day, to work out what to do.

"I got to the café where Colin, Ashley and Isaac were waiting. The letter was in the middle of the table and Mrs M and Mr M were still serving customers. They stayed busy leading up to the funeral of Levi. They had a few days to themselves. They said that I was still welcome. In fact, they wanted me to visit as often as possible. I was still family.

"Colin was the first to read it, his eyes scanning over each of the letters. He sighed, and he stared at the floor as if he didn't know what to say. Ashley was reading it over his shoulder and tears sprang from her eyes. Isaac moved the letter, clearing his throat as he looked it over. Sarah joined us eventually and looked at the letter. Once again, her arms wrapped around me with tears in her eyes. It wasn't long before they realised I was already crying, covering my eyes. Ashley and Isaac wrapped me up in a hug as I sobbed. Colin stayed sat in his seat, rubbing my back. 'You have to respond and tell them everything,' he said.

"So I did. I told the agency that Levi had died in an accident. It wasn't long before they phoned me. I spoke to them saying that there may be a chance of adopting in the future but, as of right now, it was impossible. They were understanding and that was the end of it…

"It's been years since then. I've been crushing every politician and company with everything I had. For any wrong they did, every short cut they took, I would expose them. I didn't care who they were or what they were doing. I was taking them down even if it meant doing it all day and all night. I didn't care anymore. I didn't care much about myself. It felt like I was a shell waiting to just break apart.

"My boss, Ashley, now thinks it's time my articles have a new breath of life in them. And Colin thinks it's time I move forward. Isaac and Blake encouraged me to tell you my story. They told me it was time, and that it would do me good, I think. They're not wrong, but—"

Dominic looks at the picture of Levi and him laughing and smiling that he had laid out on the table to show Arnold.

"Levi was someone who will be in your heart forever," Arnold says, filling in the pause as he listens intently. He doesn't interrupt as Dominic reaches for another tissue from the box Arnold had handed over as he had been telling his story. Dominic waits for Arnold to start telling his story. However, Arnold gives a gentle smile.

"Would you like to take a walk around the garden with me?" Dominic nods as he looks at Arnold form behind the tissue he was using.

Chapter 6

Arnold takes Dominic through the back door. As he opens the door, the cool air hits Dominic's red cheeks. Arnold starts to make his way around the garden, his hands behind his back as he walks with Dominic by his side. "I like flowers, not gardening," he says factually as he looks around him. Up against the walls are small rose bushes, and the colour of cheeky pink and gentle white petals delicately fall to the floor. Next to them is honeysuckle that climbs the wire that clings to the safety of the fence.

Arnold stops when he comes across the wider part of the garden. It looks over into a field that stretches over into a little valley filled with glowing yellow flowers. "In the early mornings, when the flowers aren't in bloom and the sun catches just the top of the grass, you can see the morning dew in the winter. Now you can catch sight of deer and nesting birds, and if you're lucky, the rabbits and badgers." Arnold speaks while chuckling at the memory. "I like the smell of the honeysuckle when it's in full bloom," Arnold says, pointing to it before he leads Dominic further down the garden path. Dominic watches the honeybees hum as they work on the flowers in the afternoon sun as he walks with Arnold.

"The hedgehogs love the slugs and the hidden boxes, especially when I chuck loads of freshly cut grass on top. And up there is a crow that nests in an old oak tree. He collects shiny things and it's funny when the three hags start complaining. Just last week, he stole Ms Snow's silver earrings." Arnold laughs. "She doesn't even wear earrings."

He stops at a bench made from walnut. The arms are of a black pristine iron that wildly twist and turn as they join with the legs in the middle, which are in the shapes of grapes and blackberries along the curls. Proudly in the middle, there sits a silver plate on the bench that reads, *In loving memory of Madeleine Hopkins.*

"Madeline Hopkins, who was she?" Dominic asks Arnold. Arnold sits on the bench, tapping the empty space beside him.

"She was the most sassy, loud, jolly, and intelligent woman who I had the privilege of knowing, is what she would've said. She was my best friend in here," he says while chuckling. "She was my rock, and I was hers. We both had something in common and we made the most of what time we had left." Dominic nods as he listens.

"So, after I listened to your story, I think it is only right that I tell you mine." Arnold speaks as he nods his head.

"I would hope so. That was what we agreed on." Dominic laughs slightly.

Arnold laughs and shakes his head, "I don't ever remember saying I would tell you. I just said I'll see you tomorrow." They burst out laughing. "Before I do. I will give you a piece of advice." Arnold says, his voice suddenly very serious.

"In life, things never seem to go the way you want them to. But, you should never stop moving forward. Take what memories you have of the past and use them to build the future. The present is something too complicated to unravel, as pleasant as it is. The present is a time where no regrets should be made. And the future is what you build using the blocks of the past as a mould." Every word is carefully remembered. Arnold looks to the bench and continues. "But, one thing is for sure. When it comes to life advice, no one really knows what they're doing, and if they tell you differently, they're lying." Dominic chuckles as Arnold looks to him with a look that causes them both to laugh.

"Madeline used to give two pieces of advice all the time when her grandchildren came around. The first one was how people treat you is their karma, and how you react is yours. The next one was that even though time is continuously ticking, never take a second for granted. The next chapter of your life starts with a step forward and a single brave action," Arnold says, smiling as he recalls his dear old friend's words. Dominic nods as he listens to the advice given. He has heard the first one before.

Dominic notices that Arnold has been smiling non-stop. "Why are you suddenly so jolly?" Dominic questions, tilting his head ever so slightly.

"Well, tomorrow is Thursday and I get to see my wife," Arnold says in excitement, looking round the garden in good spirits.

"I see," Dominic says, unsure of what else to say. "How about on Friday? Can I come and listen to your story then?"

"Yeah, that would be nice. And next time I visit her you can come," Arnold says, Dominic smiles and nods in agreement.

With that, Dominic leaves saying goodbye and Arnold can't wait for Thursday to come.

Thursday morning arrives with the birds singing and the sun shining.

Arnold's radio clock chimes, "Good morning, the time is eight thirty a.m., this is Sunshine FM, and the weather today is sunshine and dry with a bit of cloud later this afternoon. The temperature is expected to be between 15 and 19 °C, dropping to 12 °C in the evening with no signs of showers. So, for any of—"

Arnold leans over and switches it off, a grin plastered on his face.

Arnold walks to his washing basin that sits in the corner of the room. The tiles are white with deep blue triangles in the middle. Turning the taps on, the water begins running happily into the sink. The once clear water soon turns into soapy after he washes his face and pits. After unplugging the sink, Arnold grabs his toothbrush and starts cleaning his teeth. After a couple of minutes he finishes up. Picking up a brush, he starts humming to himself as he brushes his fluffy white hair. His eyes twinkle as he examines his clean shaved face in the mirror, not a stubble in sight, he smiles as he thinks he should have them more often, "They did a good job yesterday," he says to himself. As he gives the mirror a quick wipe, Arnold can see his reflection and with a satisfied nod he makes his way to the wardrobe.

Arnold opens the doors. There are jumpers, vests, trousers, hats, ties, suits in bags, and his everyday clothes, but today he reaches for one of his bags. With a gentle hand he strokes each of the bags. "I'll go with you today I think, Charles," he says in whisper.

Placing the suit upon the wardrobe door, he opens his sock drawer and picks a pair of red socks. Arnold smiles as he gently pulls them through his hand. Placing them on the bed he looks to his ties and pauses. "Ah," he thinks.

As Arnold gets dressed, he looks to his chest of drawers that sits just next door to the wardrobe. On the top is a lace cloth that settles upon the beautifully varnished walnut wood. As Arnold buttons his shirt, he smiles at the picture that decorates the chest of drawers. It's of a woman whose skin is as beautiful and deep as hazel. Her hair is as black as night with a subtle wave and reaches the middle of her back in length. Her eyes are a deep and piercing dark brown – almost black – that pierce every soul with their twinkling beauty. When she smiles, the dimples on her right cheek show. Arnold sighs as he looks at the photos. "Oh, Tallulah. I'll be seeing you soon."

There's a knock at his door. "Arnold, you ready yet?" calls a voice he knows all too well. It's his nurse Steven, a strong lad. Steven tall, helpful and quick witted which Arnold reckons comes from his family.

"Steven? I need your help picking a tie," he calls out to Steven. It isn't long before he comes in. In his hands is a bouquet of flowers, a picnic basket, and a blanket.

"Wow, look at you, Arnold," he says with a big grin. Arnold smiles as he looks to Steven, who approves his very dapper friend. Patient. Steven smiles and looks at his collection of ties. He has blue ones with purple triangles, striped ones, plain ones; too many to choose from.

"What socks are you wearing today, Arnold?" Steven asks as he looks through the many ties.

"Red," Arnold replies, lifting his trouser leg to show him the socks. Steven nods and picks out a tie that's red with black lines. He picks a rose pin, pinning it in the middle of the tie to keep the back of the tie in place.

"There. Now you look perfect," Steven says with a smile.

Arnold picks up his long coat and hat. As he puts them on, he turns to look at the mirror for one last look. Suit he got from his adoptive parents, was Charlie suit. A suit he wore when he met Tallulah. It's a dark grey suit and the shirt is white and red checked, accompanied by the tie picked out by Steven with the small rose pin that sits there well. Perfectly. The dark grey woolly long coat is hooked through his arm, as well as a hat that sits on his head proudly. Arnold can't help but grin.

"Can't keep Tallulah waiting," he says, looking to Steven

through the reflection. Steven nods. Picking the picnic basket and blanket up from the bed he leaves the room, leaving the flowers for Arnold to pick up.

"I can't wait to see you, Mrs Lovelock."

Meanwhile, at Hedgehog care hospice, Tallulah Lovelock opens her eyes as a small bit of sunlight strokes her wrinkled, fair, and hazel skin. Her short, silver, and wavy hair is messy from sleep. Refusing gravity as she lifts her head, a small yawn leaves her mouth.

A knock is heard at the door, "Tallulah? It's Nurse Emily, I'm coming in." A smile graces Tallulah's features.

"Good morning," she says. Emily returns the smile and looks to her as she stares at the window. "The weather is lovely today. Do you think Arnold will be happy again? Or do you think he's forgotten me?" she asks Emily as she starts getting out of bed. Emily shakes her head and chuckles slightly.

"That man is head over heels for you, my dear. Now wash yourself up, the dress is on the bed ready. Call me if you need any help – I will be outside the door," Emily says with a big smile on her face. Tallulah returns the smile and makes her way to the bathroom.

Emily stands outside waiting when she can hear a handful of nurses wittering on. "It's Thursday, isn't it?" one questions.

"Yes, so Emily and silent Kyle will be going with Tallulah Lovelock today," another reminds her as she makes a light clanking noise with a spoon.

"Oh yeah, to see her husband. I didn't think that was true!" another nurse says out of shock.

"Yes. You're new, but you'll find that Mrs Lovelock is quite the unusual patient. She has her moments where things are going fine but then can be quite violent. A miracle happens every

Thursday, she remembers her husband, her life and her love. But just like Cinderella's ball ended it midnight. Tallulah's ends just as their day together does. The head nurse says in a meaningful tone.

"Wow, they must really love each other." The new nurse sighs. The head nurse simply nods and the conversation continues on with how the rest of the day is going ahead.

"Emily?" came Tallulah's voice. Emily immediately goes into the room. Tallulah stands there holding a hairbrush and wearing her dress inside out. Emily gives a small smile.

"Oh dear, what's happened?"

"I—I don't remember how to use this," she says in a small voice. Emily gives her a smile that helps her worries melt away.

"Not to worry," she says, "but first let's fix the dress, shall we?" Tallulah looks up and down before giving a small nod.

After the dress is fixed, Emily helps Tallulah with her hair. She put a bit of volume to it and tries to style it by brushing it inwards using a wax to keep the curls and waves in place. The dress is white with blue flowers at the bottom that have small butterflies amongst them. The dress has a dark blue sash that gently sits on her waist. She holds a blue sunhat and dark sunglasses while carrying a small handbag. On her neck is a locket with A and T engraved in such a beautiful flower design, and inside are two pictures. On one side is a picture of them when they were young and on the other is picture of them on their wedding day.

Tallulah did a little spin in the mirror. "Wow," she whispers.

"You look beautiful," Emily says with a smile. "You ready to go?" Tallulah nods excitedly as she slips on her shoes. Emily places the Velcro across, making sure it isn't too tight or too loose.

Tallulah looks up as Kyle enters the room. He nods and gives her the thumbs up. "Oh, Kyle." Tallulah smiles as she rummages through her bag and gives him a hard candy. Kyle smiles and places it into his mouth. The cherry flavour wraps his taste buds in the flavour, making him smile at the taste. Emily simply rolls her eyes.

Emily picks up her phone from her pocket and sends a message to Steven to let him know that Kyle and herself are on their way to the meeting point.

Arnold is sitting on a bench staring at the gazebo where some musicians are playing songs. They are always there on Thursdays and Arnold always listens to them, tipping them handsomely in their instrument cases. Arnold has become one of their favourite patrons and their biggest fan.

Arnold gives them a little wave and is returned with a smile and a nod. The music fills the park with such gusto and happiness that most who hear can't help but smile and tap their feet or fingers to the beat.

Arnold bolts to his feet when he sees three figures making their way through the green grass, where children are playing a game of tag. Other couples are walking, sharing music from their phones or looking at their phones. But the three he recognises put a spring in his step. He waves his hand wildly.

Tallulah spots him and waves just as excitedly back. "I see him," she announces with glee. Emily smiles and nods, giving her the little encouragement she needs to almost run to him.

Arnold runs to her, opening his arms as she runs into them. "Arnold." She sighs into his chest, his smell filling her nostrils and helping her relax.

"Tallulah," he says, giving her a kiss on the head, then the

81

cheeks, and finally on the lips.

Taking her by the hand, he makes his way to the setup he has in place. "You look beautiful as ever." He smiles, giving her the bouquet of flowers.

"Oh, Arnold," Tallulah cries in surprise. She gently takes them and smells them. "And you haven't aged," she says, placing her hand on his cheek.

The nurses meet up in the middle and make their way to the café and watch them. "Emily. Kyle." Steven greets them with a smile as he continues to watch Arnold and Tallulah.

"Steven." Emily returns the greeting as she orders their drinks. Kyle simply gives a grunt.

"Kyle, do you ever speak?" Steven asks as he stares at the quiet giant, who simply smiles and nods.

Emily rolls her eyes. The waiter brings their drinks and leaves them on the table. "What have you been doing then?" Emily asks Steven. Steven doesn't take his eyes off Arnold and Tallulah.

"Well, we've been talking to some reporters about the home, and Mr Wolf has taken an interest in Arnold." As Steven sips his drink a satisfied hum escapes his lips. He continues to drink every now and then,

"Mr Wolf! As in the man who wrote all the articles that brought down companies and targeted many people? I'm sure there was better way of doing it. Think of the families!" Emily sounds disgusted. Steven stops drinking and looks at her from the side.

"You didn't hear? Did you?" he asks, even more shocked, "the companies he went for were dodgy in some way. And the workers who didn't know were found jobs elsewhere." Emily rolled her eyes still in a strop she leaned into her chair, "It's not

my place. But what I will say is that Mr Wolf is not a bad guy."
Emily glares at nothing in particular as she turns her head away.
As the sun enjoys the company of the light blue sky with the odd
decorative white cloud drifting by, Arnold places the contents of
the picnic basket onto the blanket. He watches Tallulah smile and
lick her lips at the sandwiches. "Dig in." He chuckles. Tallulah
isn't shy about what she wants. She picks up two ham
sandwiches, five mini sausages, and a couple of cheese cubes
with a packet of crisps. The fluff of the bread in her hand and the
smell of ham is intoxicating and it doesn't take her long before
she takes a bite. She closes her eyes as the flavour fills her mouth.
"This is good," she says. Arnold rolls his eyes; her habit of
speaking with her mouthful hasn't changed.

Arnold pours her a drink of elderflower and sparkling water
with the bubbles fizzing to the top. The sizzling noise fills her
ears as he hands her the cup. "Thank you." She smiles and Arnold
leans back and enjoys picking at random bits of food that lay on
the blanket. All he wants to do is gaze at Tallulah.

"What?" she asks suspiciously. Arnold shakes his head with
a shy smile that spreads on his face. He's been caught staring,
and a slight blush plays on his ears, causing him to look away
slightly. "After we've eaten, would you like to take a small
walk?" Tallulah asks him. Arnold looks up. This is different;
she's never asked before now. He nods happily and is excited at
the change. Tallulah and Arnold start packing the food away into
the basket.

The clattering of plates is a nice sound to them. "Do you
remember our home?" she asks him suddenly. Arnold is taken by
surprise and doesn't know what to say. Tallulah continues. "I do.
The smell of lavender when we came to the door. The red roses
on the window." She speaks clearly as she carefully places the

plates in the basket. "The way the carpet felt under my feet felt like it was new every day. The colour of the walls." She pauses as she tries to remember.

Arnold smiles. "They were a blush pink with a gentle lavender going into a pale blue," he says, helping Tallulah up onto her feet and leaving his coat and hat on the basket so they remember where their spot is.

Tallulah smiles and kisses his cheek and he pulls her arm through his. They start walking round the edge and he starts to hum a tune.

"Oh, Arnold, a band!" Tallulah shouts with glee as she notices the group that are playing by the gazebo. "You don't think this gazebo is still the same?" Arnold chuckles and nods to her question. Tallulah stops briefly as Arnold walks over and asks them to play a piece of music.

"Hey guys, could you play what you played the last time I was here?" Arnold asks, smiling. The man with violin smiles back.

"For your old timer, anything. It's our cover for 'Silhouette'."

Arnold nods at his response. "Thank you."

Arnold holds out his hand after taking off his suit jacket and throwing it on the grass. "May I have this dance?" he asks with his cheeky smile. Tallulah nods and, taking his hand, her fingertips to his slowly glide into his palm as they reach his wrist. Arnold pulls her by the waist and their feet begin to move on their own.

As the music begins to lift, the keyboard is the first to play. The vocals are soft and graceful, blocking out any other noise, and it's like they are in their teens or early twenties again, taken to a room with just them. The violin began and soon the bass drops. Arnold begins spinning her around in his arms, pulling her close and far, never taking his eyes off her. Tallulah's dress is perfect for dancing today; light and not too heavy for her. They did a waltz, almost going into a slow fox trot, if such a thing exists. They are spell bound by the music and each other. Arnold still lifts her, and as she holds onto his shoulders, she giggles like she did all those other times. Their silhouettes cross each other in the sun as they merge.

As the song slows down, Arnold pulls Tallulah close, tightly holding her, as he remembers his first dance with her the dress she wore, the way she had her hair half up and half down. Their first wedding dance, he held her close like this. Time just seemed to slow for them.

"I love you," he whispers, sweetly.

"I love you, too," Tallulah whispers back. Arnold twirls her once again and dances with her, her back against his chest, as if the act has brought them back to reality they are really in.

As the song finishes, a burst of claps erupts from the people watching in awe. The musicians are used to the dancing that they did; it's always different, but the past few weeks it's been the same song.

Arnold looks at Tallulah who gives a little wave and looks to him shyly. "You've still got it," he says with a smile. Tallulah gives him a little push.

"You were slow," she mocks. Arnold watches as she starts to walk on a little, going to thank and chat to the musicians. As he does, he starts to notice that his chest tightens slightly in pain. He reaches into his pocket and takes out a little silver tin, taking out a pill and swallowing quickly without anyone seeing. The pain eventually subsides, but to his dismay there is still a bit of discomfort.

"Tallulah, are you ready?" Arnold calls to her, making his way over to her, picking up his jacket along the way which is now scrunched in the crook of his arm.

"Oh, yes," she says. Remembering that time stands against her, she waves goodbye to the musicians. Tallulah holds onto Arnold as they chat about nothing and everything. And time goes by in a flash.

"I don't want to go," Tallulah says in a hushed tone. Tinted in pain, Arnold feels the same but he has to let her go; she needs to go.

"I love you, no matter what," he says. Wrapping her in his arms she holds her arms around him, nuzzling her face into his chest.

"I'm scared. I feel like a stranger in my own head. My own reflection is a stranger," she whispers.

Arnold closes his eyes, his heart screaming not to let go, to run back home where they can be together all the time. "I know, it's scary. But, Tallulah, they're looking after you properly. Better than I ever could," he says, his eyes clenching shut, hating every word leaving his mouth. "I will always love you, no matter how many times you forget me. I'll just make you love me all over again. If you forget who you are, I'll remind you how amazing you are," he says opening his eyes. Arnold gently pulls her to him, cupping her face and wiping away the tears that escape.

"Please don't cry," Arnold says, kissing her cheeks. "My Tallulah, my mighty Tallulah." She laughs a little before a smile finally graces her features. With a nod of satisfaction, she kisses his hands and cheeks.

"Don't get old now," she says and Arnold laughs.

"Don't get younger," he responds.

Emily and Kyle soon leave with Tallulah and the park feels

less bright and exciting.

"Arnold?" Steven says, standing next to him holding the basket, blanket, his coat, and his hat. Arnold nods.

"Shall we go to the pub?" Arnold asks him as he takes his hat and coat. Before Steven can protest, Arnold is already leaving.

Much to Steven's surprise, the pub is quiet. "Steven, I need you to do something for me," Arnold says, looking at him dead in the eye. Steven doesn't like it when Arnold gets serious.

"I don't like where this is going," Steven says.

"Mr Wolf and I have an agreement. He will be coming with me on a couple of my visits with Tallulah, and he promises not to interfere. Mr Wolf is bringing his colleague Blake to take photos and Colin will also be attending here and there, as usual. But I have another matter I wish to discuss. It's the matter about my will," Arnold says as he takes a sip from the cider he ordered a while ago. They make their way to a table. After seated comfortably Arnold begin to talk. "Steven. On the occasion of my death don't be shocked when you suddenly receive something 'big' you see in only know little thing about my life, and one of them is that you have stood by me through it all. Also I've made sure that if I am to die first before Tallulah that her treatment is still paid for." Steven takes small sips from his drink as he listens to this dark topic.

"We had a son once. But he died at birth so weren't allowed to see him." Steven looked at him a strange look fell across his face. "That doesn't sound right" he said. Arnold shrugged before picking his drink up, "back in my day it was very different."

Arnold looked like he suddenly remembered something, "Mr Wolf will be working with me then observing you? Emily has to agree to it, but I don't think she'll protest too much. As for

87

you will, I have already told you, I'm flattered, but—" "Steven!" Arnold yells slightly, causing Steven to jump. "It's done." Steven falls into his chair and Arnold sips his cider. Steven stares at him. "Yes, Mr Wolf. I mean Dominic will be joining you. there is supposed to be another joining. I believe his full name is Blake Evans." Steven nods as he listens. They fall into a quiet lull, a comfy silence that often happens between the two. Arnold speaks first.

"You know, Tallulah is the first girl I ever dated. Her father owned the pub down the road from where I lived. Lovely man. She has five brothers. Marcus, John, Simon – then it was Tallulah – Matthew, and Jedidiah." He smiles as he remembers the memory. "It was a time when even after the war, after everything we as people went through, people still treated others differently. Women were treated as if they couldn't do anything and people with black skin would still receive the odd look, comment, or even be wrongly accused of crimes or get attacked." Arnold's voice is soaked in disgust. Shaking his head, he knew even though there have been new laws since then, times haven't changed. He wished people understood that, at the end of the day, everyone is the same. Arnold hates people and how they treat each other. Life would be so much simpler if everyone treated each other with respect and with equal understanding, not all this nonsense he sees in the news. Arnold is a rare man these days.

"I was young, and I didn't agree with it. At school I would sit with them, on the bus I would sit with them, and when I knew I was in love with her – well, that was it. With Tallulah, I told the whole world. I climbed the biggest hill and shouted at the top of my voice with her by my side." Arnold chuckles slightly as he opens his wallet, showing Steven a picture of him and Tallulah in walking gear soaked to the skin with grins on their faces. Steven can't help but smile with him. Arnold continues. "But, what I don't understand is why she has to be taken away from me. I don't want to let go. I just want to go home. With her." Steven listens to Arnold choke slightly as he talks about himself for the first time in all the years he's known him.

"I know it's hard and you're struggling. It's the first time you've spoken about her like that with me," Steven says, looking at Arnold who wipes his eyes and sniffs, nodding and clearing his throat.

"Shall we head off soon?" he asks. He stands up, leaving Steven with a slight smile on his face.

Chapter 7

Friday comes in a flash. Dominic is sitting in the garden where Arnold took him before, admiring the stillness and the breeze blowing the flowers as if they are waving at him. In Dominic's hands is a bag of homemade cakes that Mrs M had given him to take.

Arnold comes to the garden followed by Steven with a table and some chairs. Dominic stands and rushes over to help.

"Ah, Mr Wolf, this is Steven, my dear friend and nurse. He will be accompanying me." Dominic smiles after putting the chairs and table in place and shakes his hand.

"Nice to meet you, Steven," Dominic says. Steven nods.

"I understand you're talking to Arnold about his life?" he asks.

Dominic nods his head slightly. "Yeah, along those lines. I'm mainly focusing on the moment he knew he was in love. The moment everyone thinks 'Ah, they're the one,' where everything else kind of follows along with it." Dominic grins slightly. Steven nods his head.

"I've read all your articles. Why have you suddenly decided to write this now?" Steven asks, slightly narrowing his eyes as he crosses his arms in front of him. Arnold lowers himself down in the chair as the two men seem to stand closer together.

"I think it's time to. Time for me to move on," Dominic says proudly, almost to himself as he clenches his hands in a tight fist.

"We ready then?" Arnold asks him. Dominic nods his head

as he moves away from Steven sitting in front of him.

"So, where do we start?" Arnold asks. Dominic looks at his watch and brings out a tape recorder, a note pad, and a container full of goodies.

"I'll introduce everyone and then we'll just chat. The recorder is there to record the conversation and the note pad is for me to jot down things when I want to take notes." Arnold nods.

Steven looks at Dominic and then notices Blake start to jog over. "I'm sorry I'm late." He's panting hard.

"Ah, yes. I forgot you'd be joining us. This is Blake Evans," Arnold says, introducing Blake to Steven.

"He's the photographer?" Steven asks. Dominic nods in confirmation and Blake sits down and looks around the table. The atmosphere is relaxed; it's not one he is used to like in other interviews. He found those slightly tense and made him on edge in the professional environment.

"Let's start. It's Dominic Wolf, with good old Arnold Lovelock and his nurse, Steven. Blake Evans is here as well with photography." The tape recorder has been switched on and Blake moves slightly in his chair.

"Tell me everything about you, Tallulah, and yourselves," Dominic says with a smile, making everyone relax. Arnold pulls out pictures from his photo album as he begins to recall his life, his family, his Tallulah, her family, and them.

Steven has poured tea and coffee for each of them, and Arnold makes himself comfortable. Dominic looks at the photos and smiles. Each smile grows with warmth and he grows tearful at a couple of pictures.

"Where shall I start when I talk about myself?" Arnold elderly deep voice carries a weight. Dominic looks at the table that has now been laid out with photos.

"How about from the beginning?" Arnolds smiles as he looks to the picture in Dominics hand.

"Well, I was born in 1933. I lived in a house with a black door and I remember the sound of the bombs being dropped when I was five. It was a scary time, World War Two," Arnold says, looking sad. "My best friend and I were collecting shrapnel when we were eight maybe nine, so this was around 1946 1942, and that's when I met her, Tallulah." Arnold smiles as he pulls out a photo of kids grinning with mud and dirt all over their knees. "To this day I will never forget it. She began to slip backwards into a hole while one of her brothers wasn't looking." Arnold strokes at the photo. "I caught her hand and said to her, 'Got you, so don't let go.'" Arnold looks at Dominic and Steven. "I said, 'My name's Arnold Lovelock, what's yours?'" Arnold smiles at the recollection. "She told me she wasn't telling and she walked away before turning around and shouting, 'My name is Tallulah Hall!'"

He begins to reminisce on his life.

Arnold went to school with Tallulah and her brothers at St Peter and Paul's. It's a boy's school and the girl's school was just next door. The boys would hang out together by the fence.

Arnold lets out a hearty laugh as he points at a picture of himself surrounded by Tallulah's brothers. "I was fourteen in this picture. I told them that I was in love with Tallulah," he says, pointing to himself in the photo. "They didn't believe me because of how old I was." Arnold's smile begins to fade.

He sees a picture of his parents with smiles on their faces, his father holding him tight. "Arnold?" Dominic holds his shoulder as he reading his face, each wrinkle that showed the emotion he'd seen many times before when people looked at

92

photos of loved ones that aren't around anymore.

"Tallulah's dad was called Reginald. The pub he owned was good and many loved going there, but it didn't mean that some of the people didn't like the fact that he was able to own it." Arnold says, almost looking angry. "When my father came back from the war he wasn't the same man. He had a stronger sense of what was right and wrong and how people treated others. But it was like violence was just his way of doing things. He became a police officer and looked after a lot of people, but in the end, it ended him." Arnold's hands tighten.

When the scene of Reginald being punched plays in Arnold's head, Arnold remembers how he tried to help. Arnold ran pulling some of the men off him, punching them and pushing them away. The drunken idiots. When the police whistled and shouted, "Arnold, go," Reginald grunted and Arnold shook his head as he helped him up, checking him over.

He remembers he heard his dad's voice. "Arnold? Reginald? You all right?" he'd asked. Arnold remembers his father picking Reginald up and taking him in to the pub, where he found the drunks battered and bruised, getting up from the floor and ready to strike again.

"Right, lads, you've had enough to drink, and you're going down to the station!" Arnold remembers the anger in his father's voice. "Arnold! What do you think you were doing? Go home, go straight to your room, and I will discuss this with you tomorrow." Before Arnold could retaliate his father walked away, shoving the men out the door making them stumble over their feet. With the other police officers catching them.

Marcus came into the pub and helped his father upstairs when John sat next to Arnold. "He's just doing his job," he told him. Arnold's face was still a face of thunder. John laughed a little and grabbed his shoulders. "You've got what it takes to look after Tallulah, that's for sure. You're what, seventeen now?" Arnold nodded. "Don't worry about it, he may say good job tomorrow." John stood up and left Arnold to simmer down a little.

It wasn't long before he made his way to the door when he could hear footsteps running down the stairs. "Arnold." It was Tallulah's voice. Arnold didn't turn around. "Thank you." She spoke meaningfully. Arnold nodded, his back still facing her, and left the pub.

Dominic listens to the story. "You didn't turn around? She didn't kiss you? What did your father say to you?" A bombardment of questions. Even Steven nods as he listens and Blake smiles, his camera resting on his lap. Arnold chuckles as he recalls the next day. His father smacked him hard on the side of the head, then gave him a massive hug.

"He told me to not put myself in danger and that his heart nearly stopped beating." Steven and Dominic lean backwards and smile. Blake takes a picture of the three of them.

Dominic realises Arnold hasn't said anything about his mother, there was a picture of Tallulah by a headstone, holding some flowers, another one of both Arnold and Tallulah on the back on the photo was Fathers death. Dominic looked to Arnold who was smiling at some the pictures that looked like they hadn't been seen since they went into the photo album. Arnold pull another picture.

"Last day of school, I finally asked her out. I had the courage to ask her to be my girlfriend. And she said yes." Dominic smiles as he listens. "And that's the moment I knew I was going to marry her." Dominic nods as he watches Arnold grin at the memory. Arnold looks over at the window, and he notices most of the nurses and the rest of the residents pressing themselves against the window, grinning and waving at them. "Oh, boy." Arnold shakes his head as he slowly rises from his chair, "I will tell you more tomorrow."

"Is it okay if I borrow the pictures?" Dominic asks as he picks up four from the table.

"Just these ones." Arnold studies them in his hands: one of when he first met Tallulah, one of him and Tallulah's brothers, one from the last day of school, and another of when he proposed to Tallulah. Arnold nods and smiles.

"I promise you'll get them back tomorrow," Dominic says.

Blake smiles as he sees a grin on Dominic's face. "You look fired up." Blake raises an eyebrow. Dominic looks at him.

"You have no idea." A small dimple reveals itself on his left cheek and Blake is taken back by the expression. Standing behind him is Colin, grinning.

"He's back," Colin whispers to Blake.

"That's the look he gets when he's found something he wants to write." Colin speaks proudly as he pats Blake on the shoulder. Blake looks up to Colin then back to Dominic as he begins clearing the table whilst chatting to Steven.

Noticing how Steven and Dominic stumble around each other just before shaking hands and exchanging numbers, Blake's face clouds a little.

"Jealous?" Colin asks. Blake shakes his head quickly and Colin chuckles and pats his shoulder one last time. "You're going back to his tonight, aren't you?" Colin questions with a knowing smile.

"No. I couldn't possibly do that." Blake looks at Colin wide eyes

"Really? Oh, that's a shame, I was hoping you would," Dominic says, looking like a wounded puppy. Blake glares at

Colin who gestures to himself innocently.

"Yeah, I'll come," Blake says happily. Dominic smiles.

"Good, I'm glad you changed your mind." Dominic looks at Colin with an amused smile.

"Colin, since you're going back to work can you put this on my desk. Thanks, you're a pal." Dominic dumps all his equipment on him and quickly leaves while pulling Blake along with him. "That—I can't believe he did that. I'll hold on to it... he's going there anyway, the idiot. He owes me big time." Colin shakes his head despite the smile spreading across his lips.

Blake and Dominic are in the car driving past the beautiful scenery and Blake looks back every now and then.

"Don't worry about him, his cousin will pick him up." Dominic chuckles as he changes gear. Blake nods and begins to relax as he starts to feel less guilty leaving Colin there.

It's a pleasant trip back as Blake sneaks glances at Dominic, studying his clean shaved chin and healthier complexion. "Here we go. Before we go to the office, we're stopping here for a bit. I took the longer route," Dominic says, unclipping his seat belt. Blake looks out of the driver's window to find a building he's seen a couple of times in passing.

"Where are we?" he asks, unsure of whether he really should follow.

"Hurry up, it's my place," Dominic says, looking back into the car.

"Oh," Blake says in amazement. The building is beautiful and out of place in the street in which it stands. Its Victorian characteristics outplay all the flats that surround it. Its delicate blue is breath-taking, as are the black of the wooden beams that define the door.

"Blake, are you coming in, or?" Dominic calls to him from

the front door.

When Blake enters, he admires lots of pictures that lay hanging on the walls: some big, some small, and some long. As he makes a right, he enters the living room where papers are littered all over the floor. Most of the papers are dated from when the accident happened. Copies of police reports, hospital reports, and paper clippings of other articles.

"Found it!" Dominic's voice rings in rejoice from another room.

Dominic enters the living room to see Blake in the middle of the mess he hasn't cleared. "Ah," is all that leaves their mouths as their eyes meet.

"I found what I was looking for," Dominic announces, clearing his throat to disrupt any uncomfortable cloud forming. "I'm sorry about the mess, it's been a while since I was last here," Dominic explains. Blake simply looks round and nods.

Blake makes his way towards him. "Did you want a hand?" he asks him. Dominic looks at him then looks back at the living room.

"Yeah. But right now, we need to go to the office," he says quietly. Dominic gives a small smile as his eyes land on a picture of Levi smiling with his parents.

Blake slowly put his hands in Dominic's and gives them a gentle squeeze. "Let's go," Dominic finally says and makes his way to the front door, still holding Blake's hand. Before leaving Dominic grabbed a box filling it with papers that he needed. Taking one last look around the room making sure he had everything. Dominic laced his fingers through Blakes. Blakes face is several shades of red by the time the reach the car.

Dominic pulls up in the car park of the office that is just behind the building and he sees the security guard just about to lock up, "Hey, Len! Hold up," he shouts out of his open window. Dominic quickly unclips his seat belt, grabs the box from the Blake and runs over, locking the car up as they go.

"Are we too late?" Blake asks Len, who just laughs.

"You're kidding? For Dominic Wolf, it's never too late."

Dominic smiles, thankful for Len's kindness over the years. "Thanks," he says.

They run past Len who holds the door open for them. They get into the lift, but before they do, Dominic takes a deep breath in and lets it out as the doors close.

Blake smiles. "This is going to be the best comeback," Blake says, looking to Dominic with a beaming smile. Dominic leans towards him, pressing his lips to his for just a second, leaving Blake dazed.

The lift doors open, and Dominic leaves with a slight smug look on his face. "Hurry up!" he calls to Blake, his cheeks a rosy red. As they run to Dominic's desk, he sits down and starts typing away at the computer about Arnold's and Tallulah's life.

Blake watches him type. Dominic is so focused he isn't even aware that three hours have already gone by. The article he is writing is on three pages of the newspaper. Blake smiles as he goes to his desk and starts to work his magic with the pictures he took, especially the ones he managed to get of them dancing, the band playing by chance unknown to Dominic.

After a while, Blake smiles when he suddenly notices a coffee appears in his view.

"Got you some coffee. Is that Arnold and Tallulah?" Dominic asks as he admires the photo from the screen.

Blake nods. "Yeah, I was there at the park yesterday doing some shots for a side project I'm doing. When I recognised Arnold, I took some sneaky shots," Blake says, smiling as he looks at the pictures. Dominic looks at them too.

"They're good, he really loves her." Dominic sounds so warm in his tone and Blake nods as he sighs.

"Yeah, he really does." Dominic pats Blake on his shoulder with a gentle smile as they stare at the photos. "They really are nice," Dominic whispers.

Dominic starts walking to his desk again as he rereads what he's written. Dominic, Blake, and Colin now have been visiting the Sunset Pearl Home for a while now, and the story that Arnold shared today is full of both sad and happy memories for both himself and Tallulah. They've all gotten close with the staff and the residents that live in the Sunset Pearl Home.

Once again, Dominic sits in front of his computer as he stares at the words that lie on the page. Satisfied with the information, he circles more notes on his pad and listens to their interview in his headphones so he doesn't miss anything out. It's getting later and Dominic's eyes are getting heavier.

"Dominic, what shall I do with the pictures I've taken?" Blake looks over to find Dominic has fallen asleep. Blake can't help but laugh and it isn't long before he too falls asleep.

This continued throughout the weekend. On Monday, they went home to sleep before returning to the home to help out and listen to more of Arnold's story. Steven and Dominic grow closer as they exchange stories of their own. Blake enjoys taking pictures of the happier environment that has grown in the home.

Without them realising, on Wednesday they worked through the night again, Colin heaved a sigh and watched as Blake stifled a yawn. This time Dominic was looking over the format of the article and how it will look in the paper. Blake smiles to himself as he watches Dominic in his element. When Dominic asks him, "Are you dating anyone?" Blake almost laughs at the question before Dominic's serious expression causes him to take a breath.

"No," he replies. Dominic smiles and looks back at the computer.

After a few clicks Blake finally hears him say, "Good." Morning comes in the blink in an eye, and the first ones to come into the office are Ashley and Colin.

"Well, isn't this cute," Ashley says as she leans over Dominic's desk. Blake has made his way to Dominic's chair and sleeps on the same desk. Colin smiles before Ashley loudly shouts, "Rise and shine!"

"I'm awake!" Dominic springs up with a paper sticking to his cheek and sticky notes on his forehead. Colin can't help but laugh when he helps Dominic take some of them off. When Blake, however, doesn't wake up, Dominic looks at him and a mischievous smirk claims his lips.

"If you don't wake up, I'll jump you right here," he whispers right into his ear, so that his lips are just brushing his ear. Blake's eyes snap open and he leaps from his seat.

"The cat did it!" he shouts. Ashley can't help but laugh.

Colin hands them a drink, a bag with a change of clothes, and breakfast.

"What time is it?" Dominic asks.

"About nine o'clock," Colin says, looking at the clock on the wall. "And it's Thursday," Colin reminds him. Dominic springs from his chair and legs it out of the office with Blake following close behind. Colin eventually follows after saying his gentle goodbye to Ashley.

Chapter 8

Dominic, Blake, and Colin are at the park where Tallulah and Arnold are dancing. Much to Emily's surprise, Steven is waving at them, causing her to spit her coffee out and Kyle to jump in his chair a little and send her a disapproving look. Dominic and Blake make their way over, shaking hands with Steven and introducing Colin. Emily looks between Dominic and Steven. "You guys know each other?" Dominic and Steven look at each other and nod.

"Yeah, through Arnold." Dominic nods towards Arnold and Tallulah, and Emily immediately frowns and sighs as she starts sipping her coffee.

"Oh, you're *him.*" Blake looks taken aback by the comment. However, Dominic is used to comments like this and he responds how he would normally.

"Yes, that's right." He smiles with a business smile. His next response would throw them off but Colin arrived first.

"I'm Colin Moretti. I work with Dominic and Blake and I decided to join them today. Sorry about the late notice," Colin says smoothly. Emily nods politely. Kyle stands up and shakes his hand. "I'll get us something to drink," Colin says, going to the café.

"I'm writing an article about Arnold and Tallulah about the beginning of their love – so their one moment, per se. Then I'll be writing about the grief I felt during the death of my husband and how that made me into a cold man. I'll also write about how

101

my moment ended and how I started a new one." Emily stops drinking and looks at him, watching Arnold and Tallulah once again dance to the musicians, "I have a new chapter of my life, a new moment beginning, thanks to him." Dominic speaks watching them, almost as if he's a new person.

Emily carries on drinking her coffee and Kyle nods. "I've always liked your articles. It's nice you're coming back." Steven looks at Kyle in shock at the comment and Dominic nods in thanks. Blake smiles as he enjoys the exchange that's happening.

"Thank you," Dominic says.

Colin returns with the drinks and sits next to Kyle and enjoys the relaxing atmosphere that the park has to offer. Blake watches too. As Arnold and Tallulah dance together, her head is on his shoulder, swaying gently with the music. "I've noticed she always wears the cherry blossom brooch. I wonder why? Do you think it was a present from Arnold?" Blake asks.

Emily looks to him. "In some cultures, it's a symbol of feeling nature, is what I've come to find."

Dominic remembers when they were talking about his life, Arnold came across a letter of what vagley read about congratulations. The letter was tucked inside an aged envelope. Arnolds face was not showing any sign of happiness it was one of sadness and pain. Dominic couldn't bring himself to ask what was wrong. And now it seems he's about to find out.

"She had a child just before they were married, but due to complications the baby died," Emily says. Blake shakes his head.

"The baby didn't die. The baby was taken." Blake picks up his bag and Emily looks at him confused.

"How could you possibly know?" Emily asks. Blake rummages through his bag looking for documents when he finds the ones he wants, pulls them out, and places them on the table.

Colin is now leaning forward looking to Dominic. This is a massive find and would need to be investigated immediately if Blake is right. "This is impossible—how on earth…" Emily trails off as she looks over the documents.

"The nuns at the time took the baby away and told her that the child died. It's documented just here," Blake says, his finger pointing to the correct parts of the documentation. "It's because she was unmarried and ended up being taken to an unregistered place of birth. Places like these were often used as human trafficking establishments," Blake explains, bringing up further documentation. Emily is in shock as tears spring to her eyes.

"How did you find all of this?" she asks as she looks through all the documentation. Dominic is also stunned at Blake's find.

"It's not hard. I was looking for my mother. It's a bit like finding a family tree but with records. When we started talking to Arnold I had some spare time and went to the library to see what else I could find that would help and came across this. My dad owns the library so it's easy getting access, and I just followed the trail from there. I asked a few people and showed them pictures. The history of recorded arrests is in there as well as in local newspapers." Emily looks in awe.

Dominic smiles as he places his hand on Blake's shoulder. "What do we do now?" Steven asks when he looks at them.

"Investigate. Then we tell Arnold," Dominic says.

"Tell me what?" Arnold asks. Kyle jumps out of his seat. Arnold looks at them then to Dominic. "I want to introduce you to Tallulah." Dominic nods as Arnold gestures to follow him. Dominic understands the importance of time and doesn't waste a second. Thursdays are important to Arnold, and after a while, they have become important to Dominic as well.

"Here he is. This is Dominic. The one I told you about?"

Arnold reminds Tallulah. Dominic shakes Tallulah's hand only to be brought into a hug.

"It's an absolute pleasure to meet you, Mr Wolf. I've heard all sorts about you and read your articles." A fraction of confusion appeared on Dominic's face but was soon replaced with a slight smile knowing that today she is remembering everything. "May I be forward with you?" Tallulah suddenly asks with a serious face.

Dominic smiles awkwardly, not sure how to take such a question. He nods as he takes her arm and starts walking, Arnold on the other side of Tallulah. "You're a young man who buries himself in articles," she starts. "But your anger in the articles is not anger, but sadness. Isn't it?" Tallulah asks.

Dominic smiles and nods. "You're right, it is. I don't know why. At first, I thought I was getting payback at anyone who did something wrong, who tried to take a short cut. But I lost myself. I got angrier and hated myself for not being there. But by the time I realise what I'd done I found myself getting hurt and angrier. I tried to find more work for myself to throw myself into. It's an endless cycle of anger and it became harder to climb out of the hole I had dug."

Tallulah tightens her grip. "He was special, wasn't he?" she asks gently.

Dominic nods. "He was someone I couldn't help falling in love with." Dominic stops and looks behind him. "But, I have a feeling that I may have another moment. A second wind." He smiles to himself. "If it's not too late."

Tallulah smiles and looks to Arnold. Letting go of Dominic, she says, "It's never too late to love. There's your first love, then like you, you have a second wind and a third heart string. But love is always surrounding you. If you have love to give, then it'll find a home," Tallulah tells Dominic with a soft smile and a

104

firm finger. "So, young man, don't give up on something that hasn't begun," she warns him. With that, Arnold walks her away, leaving Dominic thinking back to a conversation he had with Levi.

"If I died for whatever reason, what would you do?" Dominic asked as Levi sat on his lap, facing him. A smile beamed on his face.

"Cry a lot. Then I would travel the world with you next to my heart. And eventually I would fall in love again and I know I will have your blessing because—" Dominic gives him a kiss.

"Because I want you to be happy, and never sad. I want you to be loved and to love someone. Because being able to love someone is something special just as much as them loving you." Dominic smiles as Levi leans on his chest, listening to his heartbeat closing his eyes. "I know it'll be hard for you, but I want you to do the same. Because, even when someone says a glass is half empty or half full, remember that it wouldn't matter you'd have a drink in your hand. So, share my love with someone."

Dominic smiles at the memory when he looks back at Blake who is talking with the others. Walking over, he grabs his hand and with the other, grabs his cheek and kisses his lips hard and sweet.

"I like you," Dominic announces with a smile and his eyes not wavering. "So, after we're finished with this article, I'll take you out on a date. What do you say?"

Blake blinks and blushes then sighs as a smile escapes his lips. "Yes."

Dominic nods, kissing his forehead. "Good answer."

Colin can't help but clap Blake on the back. He looks to Dominic and smiles. "About time too!" Dominic simply rolls his eyes at Colin's comment.

Dominic's phone begins to ring. He looks at the screen; it's Mr M. "Hello, you al—" Dominic freezes. Looking to Colin, he signs 'hospital' using his right hand to draw a cross on his left shoulder, Colin nods, and while apologising to everyone, leaves in a hurry. Blake looks at him; Dominic has paled. Blake stands up.

"Okay, we're coming. Colin is on his way," Dominic says. Blake looks at the others as he apologises, leaving with Dominic who doesn't say a word.

"What was that about?" Emily asks looking to Steven, who simply shrugs and looks over to Arnold and Tallulah. Emily sighs as the rest of the day carries on as normal.

Colin is outside the hospital entrance waiting for Dominic and Blake to arrive. It isn't long before they do. Colin waves at them and Dominic pulls him into a hug. "How is she?" Colin is breathing hard.

"She's 'fine'. They're being difficult and won't let me in to see her because I'm not—" Colin is interrupted by a jolly voice.

"Ah, Dominic." Mr M suddenly appears from behind him and Blake looks at him in confusion. Mr M smiles. "I'm glad you came, she'll be over the moon to see you," Mr M says taking Dominic by the arm. Mr M hobbles back to the building followed by Dominic, Colin and Blake.

Blake looks to Colin, "I thought it was going to be Ashley?" he tilts his head slightly.

Colin smiles and shakes his head.

Dominic stretches his hand out behind him for Blake, after taking his hand Blake moves beside him.

Colin grins at the sight from behind them.

"Heh." Colin smirks slightly

"Everything all right, Colin?" Mr M asks he looks to Colin. Colin coughs covering up the grin that had already been spotted. When the lifts door opens, they step out onto the ward. They can hear the sound of rushing feet and the sound of machines working every now and then.

"Mrs M is sure to be happy to see your face," Mr M says while laughing as he looks to Dominic. He gently pats him on the back. "Come on." Dominic's feet are heavy as they walk into the room where Mrs M is staying.

"Oh! You came," she says, brightening up and presenting them with a pleasant smile as if they were at the café where nothing is wrong. "They said that the operation will be successful, so there won't be anything to worry about," Mrs M explains as she places her knitting needles down. Dominic notices her hands are shaking slightly.

Mr M leaves Dominic and Mrs M in the room. "We're going to get some snacks, some 'munchies' as they say," says Mr M. With that he closes the door behind him.

"Dominic, say something," she asks, almost pleading with him. It's unusual for him not to say something.

"Everything is going to be okay." He reassures her, his voice uncharacteristically soft. He sits on the edge of the bed. "You're in the right place, they're going to do their best, so—" he says, stopping for a moment and taking her hand into his. "Stop trying to put a brave face on in front of me," Dominic finally tells her, pulling her gently into his chest. Her shoulders trembling.

"When did you get so grown up?" she asks, poking fun at him through her tears.

"I've always been like this," he replies with a slight chuckle

"Lies." She squeezes him. "What if I don't wake up?" Her voice trembles.

"Then I'll start baking," Dominic threatens.

"Don't you dare! I still have the burn marks from the last time on the kitchen walls." She tells him off for even saying such a thing. They burst into laughter.

"The heart surgeon said everything will be all right, right?" Dominic says. Looking at her, she nods. "Even if you collapsed today, it's always from exhaustion?" Dominic raises an eyebrow.

107

"Well, I'd been looking for something," she says vaguely. Dominic stares at her, urging her to carry on. "I know I didn't have time to, but no matter what, I wanted to find it," she explains. She leans over to pick up her bag, only to be stopped by Dominic who helps her.

"I found it eventually stuffed in his bedroom." Dominic looks to Mrs M in confusion. "It's a box full of his letters I'd picked up and put in and just left there. I put a letter that was addressed to you from the adoption agency. I kept meaning to give it to you," she says, handing it to him.

Dominic stares at the envelope and he kisses Mrs M on the cheek. "Thank you."

With that, the others came in. Blake brings some flowers and a bar of chocolate for her to "munch" on once she's better. "We better get going," Colin says as he pats Dominic and Blake on the back. Mrs M and Mr M wave as they leave, only for them to run into a doctor.

"Ah, sorry," Blake says. Dominic freezes. The doctor they have run into is the one that had dealt with Levi from the accident and informed them of his passing.

"Mr Wolf." Her soft voice is accompanied with a smile

"Dr Grey, it's good to see you," Dominic says whilst shaking her hand, much to Colin's surprise and Dr Grey's herself.

"Are you looking after Mr and Mrs M?" he asks her. Dr Grey pushes her glasses onto her nose as they had fallen slightly after bumping into him.

"I am," she says swiftly.

Dominic nods and smiles. "Thank you. Please take care of her." Dr Grey blinks in surprise. The last time they saw each other, Dominic wasn't talkative. When he did talk, his words were full of rage and sadness, not at her, but at the world. He had assaulted some of the staff and police officers when he was trying to get to Levi; luckily no charges were brought. "I never did say

108

thank you," Dominic says, sounding small and looking at her. Dr Grey looks confused and Dominic continues. "For what you did. You did everything you could. I'm sorry it's so late," Dominic says, placing his hand out once again. Dr Grey shakes her head, takes his hand, and carries on past him.

Blake slips his hand into Dominic's, a gentle squeeze that is returned. "Right then. Home it is." Dominic nods as if he is letting go of something. Colin can't help but smile as he watches his friend's back getting bigger.

Chapter 9

Getting into the car, Colin gets a text from Ashley asking them to return to the office. "Do you know why?" Blake asks, looking to Colin. Colin shrugs as he thinks for a minute, when a reason finally comes to mind.

"Well, we did kind of leave without telling anyone where we went."

"Or it could be that she found out that we skipped work the other day," Dominic adds.

"Or that company finally did complain after all. You know, the one where I called him a small—" Colin covers Blake's ears and shakes his head.

"Or the time I didn't put the correct reference in the article and no one noticed?" Colin adds as he thinks of some more possibilities. Blake leans back into his seat and rubs his temples as he fears the sort things they could have done.

Once they arrive at the office, they can already hear Ashley shouting at people from the reception area. "Wow, that is bad," Colin says, looking up. The receptionist shakes her head at him. "Oh, no." Colin suddenly remembers.

"What?" Dominic questions, almost in fear of the answer and unsure whether he really wants to know. Colin pales at Dominic then looks to Blake to explain, they're already in front of the lift, and the shouting is getting louder.

"We forgot about the meeting with a couple of sister companies."

As the doors open, Dominic pales. "Oh."

Blake sighs as he looks at them. "You were busy and it was something unavoidable. I'm sure she'll forgive you." Colin laughs slightly.

"Possibly, if only the pregnancy didn't make her one hundred times scarier," Colin says while shuddering, remembering a restaurant that didn't have any gherkins and so the manager ended up crying and he was left apologising.

Dominic and Blake look at each other in shock for a moment, "Wait, what?" they say in union. Colin looks at the two and laughs a little.

"Didn't I tell you?" He thinks for a moment but it hits him he hasn't. "Oh."

Dominic brings him into a hug.

The news was amazing for the two best friends. Blake gives Colin a quick hug and smiles, and Colin laughs. "I have years of experience in raising a child, thanks to you, Dom." Dominic very quickly elbows him, which earns laughter from them all.

The elevator's door open. As they do all eyes fall on them. "Colin, how much trouble are we in?" Dominic asked

Colin looked to Dominic and shrugged. Colin looked in the direction of Ashley's office.

There she stood her arms folded in front of her chest, her right foot tapping aggressively as she stared at them. "Yep, we're in trouble," Colin said as he took in a deep breath. "You're late. Not only that, but you didn't even show up to one of the most important meetings we could possibly have this year!" Ashley says in frustration as she throws her hands in the air as she speaks and makes her way down the steps towards them with speed to gesture exactly how cross she is.

"So, what excuse do you have for me now?" she says,

throwing her arms in front of her chest, Blake looks down for a second as Dominic looks to Colin who sighs as he rubs his neck. "Mrs M collapsed and was rushed to hospital." Ashley's hardened expression falls as she wraps her arms around Dominic, while one hand slaps Colin every now and then while mouthing sentences to him.

"Why didn't you send me a text, idiot!" Ashley waves her arm around.

"Sorry, I wasn't thinking." Colin raises his hands.

"Use that brain of yours!" Ashley glares at Colin.

"I'm sorry to hear that. Is she okay?" Ashley turns to Dominic.

"She will be, she's made of strong stuff," Dominic says, looking over to Colin who rubs Ashley's back when she sends a side glare his way.

"Right, I have the notes of the meeting on your desks. It's just minor. Dominic, I need to talk to you," Ashley says, back into work mode after confirming everything is all right. Swiftly turning on her heels, she makes her way to her office.

Blake watches her leave. "Just like a hurricane." Colin laughs as they return to their desks.

"Transfer!" Dominic shouts in shock. Ashley nods.

"Yes, they want you to go to their branch in New York and be an assistant editor, and if you don't like the idea of being one, then they even suggested just being Head Journalist as that way you can still be out in the field."

Dominic blinks at the sudden information thrown at him. "What about Blake?" he asks, looking out the window. Ashley follows his gaze and a smile plays across her lips.

"Well, you'll be pleased to know that they offered him a transfer as well."

Dominic spins around looking at her. "Really?" Ashley nods her head.

"Yeah, they were amazed by his portfolio he did when he applied for the job here," Ashley says, her arms gently settling under her chest.

"He's really good. I've almost finished the article, and I've changed thanks to him and Arnold," Dominic says, smiling at Blake. Ashley digs him in his side

"I gave you the article in the first place. Where's my thanks?" she teases.

Dominic laughs, he smiles at her. "Thank you." Ashley pauses. She can see the change in him and nods.

"You better get cracking on the article then. Oh, regarding the transfer. You have two weeks to make a decision. You have two weeks to make your decision," Ashley informs him. Dominic nods to Ashley as he leaves her office heading straight to Blake,

"You ready?" Dominic asks.

"For what?" Blake replies, confused.

"We've got a story to tell." Dominic smiles at him and Blake can't look away. Dominic is so different from when they first met. Returning a smile, he follows Dominic into a large room. Standing there is none other than Colin with a grin.

"Took your time."

Between them is a table, a large rectangle made of glass. It is covered in papers, photos, and notes. Three laptops are seated on the table and Blake looks to Dominic. "Let's get started."

"What about the letter and the stuff I found on Arnold and Tallulah's child?" Blake asks as he sits down by the photos and notes that are sprawling over the table. "We'll have to tell him."

Colin looks at the papers in his hands hoping that everything has been gathered together.

"I think I find them and a photo as well to show him."

Dominic looks at the paper work with him giving a firm nod.

"Want me to call him, or—?" Colin asks Dominic.

Dominic thinks for just a moment before giving another firm nod of his head.

It isn't long before he's talking to someone.

"Are you always this grumpy when you answer phone calls," Colin asked annoyed with the other end of the call. The response isn't favourable. "I think you might find that being Italian has nothing to do with it!"

Dominic is focused on typing and Blake is amazed at how quick it's all coming together. He pulls out the recorder and puts on headphones, listening to the interview again while Colin is almost strangling the phone.

"Will you stop with the long-winded conversation? Can you do it or not?" Growing irritated, Colin is gripping his hands together. Blake swore he could have seen steam rising from his head. "Fine, I'll reserve you a table on whatever day of the year and at whatever time, yes. No. The name of the person we need you to find is Andrew Hall or possibly Andrew Lovelock." Colin speaks with a serious tone. When there is no response from the other end, Colin continues. "You got the name, right? Did you want anything else?" Colin asks. "No? But I can send you a picture. Dominic said he's already done it." Colin looks over to Dominic who gives a thumbs up. "Yes, Wolf. Yes, he's back. No, he's not. No, you can't talk to him. Bye." Colin hangs up on the person. Blake looks to them in confusion and Dominic snickers a little as he continues to type.

"It's not funny, why do I always have to deal with him?" Colin sighs, sulking as he sits down in the chair.

"Who was it?" Blake asks. Colin looks from Dominic to

114

Blake.

"An old friend, someone who can find anything. He's someone we ask for help on occasions with certain cases." Colin begins to explain.

"So, a hacker?" Blake asks.

Colin shakes his head. "No, but he does hack."

Blake looks at them, even more confused.

"Blake, it's probably best you don't know." Dominic sighs as he stretches. "He's a pain no matter how you look at it. Our 'friend' is known as a handyman but only few people can actually acquire his help." Dominic grins at Colin who just laughs and shakes his head.

"We're one of those 'lucky' few," Colin says, using his fingers as quotes.

Blake nods. "So, he's going to find the child—well their son?"

Dominic nods as he returns to his article. "He'll find something," he reassures Blake with a smile.

After some hours go by, Dominic manages to chop his article to a good size, putting in as much of Arnold and Tallulah's story in as possible. Blake returns with coffee and food and Colin is pushing a pen on the table, staring at his phone.

"You know, I'm not going to phone you," came a voice that makes them all turn around. There, standing in the doorway is a man and a woman. The man has sun-kissed blonde hair with eyes hidden behind sunglasses. He wears jeans and a casual jacket. The woman with him has short black hair and her eyes are a deep blue, and she wears ripped jeans and a top that reads 'Not bothered'.

"Mark, you can't keep doing that!" Colin says, clearly annoyed as he marches towards him. Mark gives a cheeky grin

115

and Dominic simply shakes his head as if used to the exchange.

Colin smiles. "Sally." She gives a friendly kiss to the cheek as Colin shows them inside the room. "Honestly, Mark, what the hell do you think you're playing at!" Colin says. Sally smiles to Dominic and nods.

"The new face," Marks says, looking to Blake over his shades. Colin shakes his head in annoyance and Sally removes the shades for him.

"Honestly, Mark." She sighs.

"I'm Blake. Nice to meet you," Blake says, introducing himself.

"We know, name's Sally, this here is Mark." Sally grins as she puts her hand out to shake Dominic's hand, he takes it with an equally bigger grin, after not seeing each other for a long time.

"It's good to see you again old man," Mark chimed as he slapped both of Colins arms.

"We found Andrew Hall," Sally smiled looking between them all. Dominic springs from his seat before slowly sitting back into it to hear more. "That's great, where?" Dominic moves forward urgently.

"Well, the information you gave us was amazing, some of original documents were destroyed in a fire. So it didn't take long. It took us a while to find the son. Andrew Hall probably didn't know who his parents are because of the fire burning all the documentation, and because he jumped from home to home. He has two kids, his wife owns a cafe in Scotland. As for Andrew he's a partner in a law firm," Mark explains, so it didn't take long to find him. Andrew Hall jumped from home to home, so it was hard to get a decent location on him. But he's married, he has two kids, his wife owns a café in Scotland, and he's a partner in a law firm," Mark explains, sitting in Dominic's lap and completely

116

ignoring the glare he is receiving from Blake. He opens a file and empties its contents out onto the table, showing them pictures of him.

"Thank you." Dominic smiles and takes the file. "I've transferred what you wanted." Mark nods to Blake. Colin marches over and grabs Mark's, ear pulling him from Dominic's lap.

"Ow, that hurts! Oh, come on, I was only playing, Colin. Come on, lay off a little!" Mark cries as he's forced to leave by the ear. "Oh, Dom." Dominic looks up. "It's good to see you back in action," Mark calls back to him from outside the room, and Sally nods.

"Yeah, so make sure you stay in touch."

With that, Sally follows Mark in the corridor where he is still begging Colin to release his ear. Colin huffs as he returns, shaking his head.

"So, that was the handyman?" Blake asks. Looking to the guys, Dominic nods. "Are you going to tell Arnold tomorrow?" Blake asks, trying to think of anything apart from 'Mark'. Blake starts staring at the file in Dominic's hand.

"Yes."

Chapter 10

Dominic is wearing a suit and holds the file in the suitcase with the recorder, notepad, pen, and documents. Blake can't take his eyes off him as Dominic straightens his jacket. Colin rolls his eyes. "You should wear a suit more often." Blake smiles and Dominic laughs.

"Do I look that different?" Dominic asks, adjusting his tie a little.

"You look like you've stepped out of a modelling magazine," Blake says, drooling slightly. Colin rolls his eyes at the exchange.

"You look amazing, Dom. Like your old self," Colin chips in. Dominic smiles at the comment as he brushes his hand down his chest, smoothing any wrinkles that remain.

Getting to Dominic's car, Colin notices there's no hesitation anymore. With proudness in his eyes, Colin sits in the back. With the car starting up, they begin their journey.

"How do you think he'll take it?" Colin asks, looking out the window as he fiddles with his phone.

"Honestly, I think he'll be shocked. But I don't think he'll waste time to see him," Dominic answers as he turns a corner,

"He'll need time to take it in," Blake states.

"He hasn't got time," Colin reminds him. Dominic looks into the rear-view mirror, his eyes staring at Colin's serious ones.

"It's a bit of a gamble."

"Play it right, Dom, it's their life," Colin warns him.

Dominic nods as they pull up to the Sunset Pearl Home. Arnold is sitting in the garden, waiting. Dominic had called ahead to let him know that he and Colin have something important to discuss. Steven smiles as he greets them at the entrance.

"Unusual for you both to be here looking so serious," he teases, when he notices Dominic is wearing a three piece suit, Colin couldn't help but smile, seeing the Dominic he knew returning.

"Is it that important you dressed up for it?" Steven asks slightly in shock and in an amused manner.

Dominic is in a serious mood. "Yes." Steven looks at him and nods. Colin looks to Dominic when he abruptly makes a decision.

"I think it should be you to tell him. Not the both of us, just you."

"It's about the child, isn't it?" Steven asks. Dominic simply nods and starts walking to where Arnold is. Blake and Colin head into the home, as soon as they were inside the nurses and residents greeted them with warm smiles.

"Mr Wolf."

"Mr Lovelock," Dominic starts. Arnold smirks at the way Dominic is dressed. "In my briefcase I have some important documentation. This regarding a delicate matter." Arnold listens as Dominic takes a seat in front of him.

"All right, well tell me then. Enough of the theatrics." Arnold begins to sound irritated and somewhat interested in what Dominic has discovered during his time with him.

"We discovered that you have a son."

"He died at birth," Arnold says, correcting the statement.

Dominic shakes his head. "He's alive. He was taken from both you and Tallulah. It was discovered that the place that

119

Tallulah gave birth in was a hot spot for human trafficking. Your son was one of the children that had been taken. The traffickers were later arrested, and your son was saved, but instead of being returned to you he was taken to a foster home. The nuns kept no documentation of who his parents were. Thanks to those 'nuns' that committed the crime, you were to never know that he was alive." Arnold tightens his fists, to the point the knuckle whiten. For a moment his face pales, before returning.

His jaw tightens in anger upon hearing the news of what happened. Minutes pass in a suffocating silence.

While processing the news that his son is alive. He can't believe his son really is alive.

"Show me," he demands, holding out his hands. They're shaking. Dominic takes his hands and gives him a soft smile.

"It's all in here, I'll leave you to read it. Tell me what you want to do afterwards." Gently placing the file in his hand, Dominic looks to Steven who sits next to Arnold, giving him a meaningful nod.

"When you're ready, come and get us." Steven couldn't help but send them a smile and nodded. As he stayed by Arnold's side.

Dominic is pacing by the window as he watches Arnold stare at the file, his back facing him so he can't read any of his facial expressions. Colin leans against the wall watching Dominic, when Blake smiles. "Stop pacing, you're going to give everyone vertigo," Blake says, looking to everyone.
Ms Pats is chatting with Ms Snow as they place yoghurts and chocolate as bets instead of money on the table.

"What are you ladies up to?" Colin calls over. Miss Woods laughs a little when Mrs Hunter takes a sip of her tea.

"Taking bets on what's going on." Colin rolls his eyes. Asking any further would be a dangerous thing. He just nods and looks to Dominic, who sits down loosening his tie.

"We just have to wait," Colin says, patting Dominic on the shoulder. Dominic nods to Colin as he stares at the floor.

A couple of hours go by and Steven comes in to get them. "I'll go alone," Dominic says with a smile.

Colin shakes his head. "I'll come with you this time," Colin says.

Blake smiles. "I'll stay and make sure no one interrupts," he says, glancing at the table with Miss Woods and the rest. "Good luck," Blake says, encouraging them with a smile.

Arnold is standing with his hands behind his back, looking at the bench he took Dominic to when he told him the best advice he ever heard.

"Arnold." Dominic calls to him.

"Andrew Hall. We named him after my father. He died in a shooting, and I was adopted by our next-door neighbours. They were kind people. Tallulah was determined to name our son after my dad." Arnold chuckles at the memory, Colin stands a little bit away from them and Dominic stands next to Arnold. "My mind isn't what it was, I think he'd be in his mid-forties. Arnold chuckles. "He looks like a mix of both of us. He's got her smile and her eyes." He smiles whilst looking at the photo from the file. "And my nose."

"Would you like to meet him?" Dominic asks him.

Arnold looks at him in shock, "I—" he pauses for less than a second. "I would, but I don't know how to do that, so—"

"Just a simple phone call. You won't need to do anything except arrive at the place you'll meet." Dominic smiles and Arnold stares at him.

"You'd do that? For me?"

Dominic nods, placing his hand on his shoulder. "Of course

121

I will." Arnold pulls Dominic into a hug. "I'll let you know what happens." Dominic smiles. "I'll phone him today, and by the afternoon we'll know." Arnold nods.

They walk back to the table. Colin nods to Arnold who places his hand on his shoulder and brings him into a hug. "We ready?" Colin asks. Arnold nods.

Dominic starts the phone call.

"Hello?" Andrew answers the phone.

"Hello, my name is Dominic Wolf. I'm a reporter for The Astro. I'm writing an article about 'One Moment'. I chose to write an article about a man called Arnold Lovelock, and I came across something rather interesting." Dominic starts to explain.

"Ah, I do recognise your name. Could you bear with me one second?" Andrew politely interrupts.

"Sure." Dominic sounds pleased that conversation is going well so far.

"Lucy, put the rat down! Your mother is supposed to be back soon, and you still need to do your room. Laura, your coffee is ready! And don't forget to walk the dogs, please. Sorry, what were you saying?" Andrew shouts, his Scottish accent sounding strong.

"Well, I discovered that he's your biological father." Dominic gets straight to the point. He knows it isn't very strategic and he holds his breath when everything goes silent. Andrew's voice breaks slightly when a few noises come through the phone. A knock on the door can be heard at the other end of the phone.

"Laura, I need to use the study for a bit," Andrew says, in a voice that sounds almost pleading. Dominic listens to him walking into the room and the door closing. He also hears curse words from Laura – something about studying and pestering – but soon enough, another door is closed too.

"Mr Hall?" Dominic checks to see if he is still there. "Are you okay?"

"Um, can you just—one second," Andrew says. Dominic can't help but smile as the voice is filled with confusion.

"My biological father? I was told that it would be impossible to find him because I was taken away at such a young age because I was constantly moving from home to home, and that there was no documentation to find or to follow."

"Ah yes, I see. I asked a friend of mine who works in the business of finding people – amongst other things – to look into the matter for me to confirm this, which is how I was able to find you using what little documentation I found during the search," Dominic explains.

"Oh. So, um… What happens now?" Andrew asks, sounding a little bewildered with the information thrown at him.

"Well, if you would like, you can meet him. This is something you can choose to do. But please think carefully about it. I can leave you to phone me back, to give you some time to think about it," Dominic suggests.

"Yes, I would like to think about it." Andrew agrees and Dominic nods into the phone.

After giving Andrew his number Dominic hangs up. He looks to Arnold. "Now, we wait," Dominic says, leaning back in his chair.

Arnold nods as he stares at the phone that sits heavily on the table.

As the hours start to tick by, Steven goes into the kitchen to get Colin, Dominic, and Arnold some coffee and snacks. Arnold doesn't touch many of the snacks as he stares at the phone, daring it to ring. Colin sips his coffee, relaxing as the coffee fills his nostrils.

Dominic stares past the phone. When he reaches for it to check the time, the phone begins to ring. Arnold jumps as he looks to Colin who stares shocked at Dominic. The timing is perfect. The number on screen is Andrew's.

"Hello. Dominic Wolf, speaking."

"Hi, it's Andrew Hall."

"Ah, yes."

"I would. I would like to meet my father if possible."

Dominic can't help but smile as he looks to Arnold, who sighs as he leans into his chair with relief. Steven walks over to the table and Dominic is still on the phone. Arnold walks over too, giving him the thumbs up.

"Yes, so we'll meet at the park. Yes, I'll bring food, supplies, photos, and such. If you could do the same that would be much appreciated," Dominic says, as he nods whilst scribbling a time and location down. Arnold comes back over and looks at the notebook.

"Thank you for phoning me, Mr Wolf, and telling me about my father. I look forward to meeting him," Andrew says on the phone.

Dominic smiles and nods. "You're welcome."

Dominic says his goodbyes and hangs up. He looks to a tearful Arnold, who is simply nodding as he wipes the corner of his eyes. Steven stands next to him and smiles and pats Arnold's shoulder. Colin can't help but grin at Arnold.

"You're going to see your boy," Colin says.

Arnold nods happily and sniffs. "I am." He chokes slightly as he clears his throat.

"I'll see you tomorrow at the park," Dominic says as he stands next to Colin.

"So soon," Steven says happily, looking to Arnold next to

him.

"I-I see, I'm looking forward to meeting him." Arnolds voice had a slight tremor, as he swallowed a lump that had formed surreal moment. His eyes looked as though tears were going to break free, however he takes the phone out of Dominic's hand. "I have one more phone call to make."

Chapter 11

Arnold is wearing his nice trousers that he brings out on special occasions, they're similar to the trousers he wears when he sees Tallulah.

Arnolds lucky warm red jumper is clean, with no single wool bobble that normally appears on many jumpers.

Brushing his hair back he picked up a flat cap, placing it firmly on his head. He looks in the mirror and smiles giving himself a nod of encouragement. "Hi."

"Hello. Hi. What's up?" Steven can't hold it in anymore and laughs as he watches Arnold practise his greeting in the mirror. "What are you doing?" he asks through his snickering.

Through a frown Arnold pulls a little on the hem of his jumper. "Saying hello. Anyway, you know it's rude to intrude on others…" he trails off, thinking of something smart to say.

Steven can't help but shake his head. "No matter what you say, it will go well. Just be yourself," Steven reminds him. Arnold nods as he picks up his photo albums and a little parcel.

As they head outside, they find Dominic smiling and leaning against his car. Arnold stares at him.

"That's your car?" Steven asks. Arnold elbows him as he sends a slight eye roll.

"You're welcome to walk there, Steven, but I'll have you know she's a classic." Arnold chuckles.

Despite the laughter to help settle the nervous air surrounding Arnold, Arnold can't help his hands shaking. Steven helps him into Dominic's car, leaning in to clip his seatbelt. "All set," he whispers with a smile.

Arnold smiles back. "I haven't been in one of these in thirty-five years." Dominic laughs as Steven sits in the back with Blake.

"Colin is making his own way there, I think," Dominic says. "If he can't make it, he'll let me know."

It isn't long before they set off. Steven sends a text to Emily to let her know how things are going.

Blake is armed with a camera and a box of tissues for the occasion. Steven notices and can't help but laugh as he grabs a few of them.

Dominic arrives at the park where children are running with kites and pet dogs, with skateboards and parents chasing them.

"I can't believe he was alive all this time," Arnold announces, sounding nervous as Steven helps him out of the car.

Dominic smiles. "Andrew is looking forward to meeting you. I could hear it in his voice. "He was told the circumstance, I asked a friend of mine who helped with the search to inform him." Dominic explains, as he notices Arnold take in a deep breath as he stared out, noticing his hands tremble as he gripped the photo album in his hands. "I know it's a bit scary. Take a deep breath, he's nervous to. But you both have a lot of catching up to do. Don't waste what little time you have—"

Dominic was about to finish when Arnold finished it for him. "Go chase the adventure where time doesn't exist or care. This is a big step for both of us," Dominic nods as he listened to Arnold.

"So you better start moving those feet of yours," Dominic nudged Arnold. Without hesitation Arnold held onto Dominics arm to steady himself as he was lead into the park.

Steven and Blake head to their usual spot by the café that sits just at the edge of the jolly, bright green grass. A gentleman sits on a bench, looking at his phone and then his watch. Dominic can't help but smile.

"Mr Hall." Andrew turns around and almost in an instant he jumps to his feet. His eyes are a lush brown, and his hair is a messy brown style. He is tall and chubby – not overly chubby – but teddy bear chubby.

"Mr Wolf…" Andrew begins as he turns to address Arnold.

"Andrew?" Arnold said his bottom lip began to shake a little as tears burst from his eyes. "My boy," Arnold cried, as he grabbed Andrew into a hug.

Andrew beside himself, couldn't help but cry silently in the embrace of his dad.

Burying his head into his shoulder he whispered, "Dad."

"Yes?"

"Dad," Andrew repeated Arnold smiled as the tears carried on, the embrace was long overdue.

Dominic and Steven who had been watching them with tears of their own, as they smile at the scene, they begin to leave them.

Ater a few minutes of crying and hugging the two separate. Taking a few breathes before they sat down.

Andrew notice's an album that sat on Arnold's lap. Noticing his gaze Arnold hand's it to him. "I brought pictures of your mum, Tallulah, and her brothers who I phoned as soon as I found out that I was meeting you," Arnold says, grumbling as he lowers himself onto the bench. Andrew eagerly sits next to him, wanting to hear more. Arnold holds out the bag filled with photo albums. Picking an album up, the heavy book opens roughly at pages of Arnold and Tallulah doing many things. Tallulah in protests, Arnold doing some car work, Arnold and Tallulah in a gazebo looking out at the view holding on to each other.

"This one." Andrew points at a photo of Arnold and Tallulah

at a train station.

"Ah, that one. Well, you see, Tallulah is an amazing dancer and this talent bloke picked her up and gave her a dream job in the big world of stars," Arnold begins. Andrew watches him as Arnold looks a little sad recalling the memory. "I thought I was supporting her dream of wanting to be a star by telling her she should go. You see, I didn't know that she had doubts about the whole thing," he explains. "As the time got closer, we ended up getting caught in this big protest that swept through the town and I let her hand go," Arnold says, regret dripping off every word. Andrew stares at the picture. Tallulah is fast asleep in Arnold's arms at the train station, and he holds her tightly.

"It took me hours to find her, but when I did, I promised myself from that moment on, I wasn't letting go of her hand ever again. I'd always find her no matter how lost she'd get. I love her. Her eyes, her soul, her hair. Her everything," he says, smiling and thinking back. Arnold strokes the picture as he hears Tallulah's voice and recalls the day.

"Oh, Arnold, you fool," she whispers as she pants hard from being pushed, pulled, and slammed, the noise of feet and shouting still audible.

"I'm not letting you go," Arnold says.

"My lovable fool." She smiles. With tears falling, Arnold picks her up and takes her to the train station bench. He makes a quick phone call in a nearby phone box and waits for her brother to pick them up.

Andrew smiles as he looks at the photo. "You guys really are meant for each other."

Arnold smiles and laughs. "Oh, Andrew, my boy. I have lots of stories to tell you."

Blake zooms in, catching photos of their exchange. The

minute details of change in the air around them can be caught with the camera and he hopes to catch them all. The reuniting of the family that Arnold thought was lost all those years ago is special, and Blake is determined to catch it all.

Andrew smiles as he brings a bag round, pulling various albums out. "I brought photos of my wedding, the birth of my kids, getting my promotion at work, and the dogs."

"I have grandchildren?" Arnold asks, gobsmacked. Andrew nods as he watches Arnold tear up a little.

"This here is the day we found out you were in Tallulah's tummy." Arnold points to a picture of Tallulah, surrounded by flowers and her brothers and her father. Andrew smiles. "I was – am – the happiest man alive that day."

Arnold strokes the photo then looks to Andrew. "Your mother, she…" Andrew looks at Arnold with a slight understanding of what he is trying to say. He places his hands on Arnold's. "She suffers with dementia. Before she went to the home, I was stubborn. I looked after her the best I could. She had lows where she didn't recognise me at all. Many police phone calls and explanations were made. It even got to a point where she would throw things, shouting at anyone and everyone. On occasions there would be violent outbursts luckily no one was hurt; when she told me that 'Arnold is on his way to pick me up,' I knew I had to find her specialist care. Her good day is Thursday. She remembers everything on this day. I don't know if it's because she had a routine or because we did everything on thursdays. This park was our spot, our special place. So this is where we come to meet every Thursday, to this park," Arnold says, looking around. Andrew nods slowly as he understands. He picks up an album and sits it on his lap, looking forward to telling everything he can to his 'dad'.

Arnold starts flipping through the pages of the album. "We had our first date here, we made up here, I proposed here. It always seemed to happen on a Thursday, and it looks as if it just sits with her." Andrew listens intently as Arnold's eyes soften as he talks.

"Do you know that when I learnt that you were alive, I went to phone her and I couldn't." His voice catches in his throat. "Our baby boy," he says, touching Andrew's cheek. "Our brave, handsome boy. You get that from your mother." Arnold smiles. Andrew smiles back.

Arnold looks behind him and walking through the gates of the park are four men. "Ah, there they are." Andrew looks behind him. The four men are smartly dressed and catch a lot of attention.

"They're your uncles." Andrew looks to Arnold, who grins. "Well, I thought I would make up for all those years. So, I asked for some back up, I thought it would be good for you to meet not just me, but your whole family." He chuckles as he waves to them.

Andrew watches them come over, still in a state of shock at how big his family has gotten.

"You must be Andrew," John says, his warm hazel eyes twinkling as he pulls Andrew into a hug. John's hair is tidy with streaks of silver, and he smiles at them both wholeheartedly. "I'm John Hall. I'm a professor at a university, but I won't bore you with too many details. I have two sons who are also looking forward to meeting you."

Simon, reaching John's shoulder, greets Andrew. His hair has silver slithers amongst his black locks and he pulls Andrew into a hug. "I'm Simon Hall."

Mathew's hair is untouched by age, seeing no white or silver.

"I'm Mathew," he says, giving Andrew another hug. As Andrew is being hugged, he starts to notice he's getting emotional.

Jedidiah is the same height as John. "I'm Jedidiah. Call me Uncle Jed or Uncle J." He grins as he looks Andrew over. "I can't believe I'm looking at our nephew. Wow," he says. He chokes a little, pulling him into a big hug.

"Okay, you lot put my son down," Arnold grumbles. Andrew looks at all of them as he begins to sniff, rubbing his eyes a little at the number of family members that have entered his life. Andrew looks to where he can see Dominic, Blake and Steven are sat. in his heart he thanks them. Without them, none of this could have been possible. Blake while watching the scene smiled and captured the happiness that radiated through the reunion in a single shot.

Andrew and his uncles are looking through the albums and exchanging numbers and addresses. Jedidiah announces, "Well, it's my turn to do Christmas this year. Why not come around and bring your family? I want to meet my great nieces." Andrew is taken back by the invitation. He looks at their faces, each smiling. Not a single one is forcing him to go.

"Do you know what? Yes, that'd be great," he says, nodding.

Jedidiah nods and pats his back. "Good."

"I'll be right back," Arnold says as he pats Andrew's shoulder too.

Arnold makes his way to Steven and Dominic. When he gets there, he notices Blake is distracted by a photo opportunity from some birds that landed close to him.

"I don't know how I can ever thank you for all of this, Dominic. You've created another moment for me," Arnold says, looking to his family that are laughing at the photos.

Dominic shakes his head. "No, I did nothing. You showed

me I could keep walking forward. There is always more to life than standing still and watching it carry on by. I have to live it and love it. Cherish the memories of the moment I have and create new ones." Dominic smiles at Arnold as he catches a glimpse of Blake smiling at his camera screen.

Arnold nods, putting his hand out for Dominic to shake. Dominic takes his outstretched hand and Arnold smiles and slowly brings him into a hug. Arnold nods to Steven. Before leaving, Arnold looks to Dominic one last time. "Thank you."

Steven accompanies him to join the family reunion. "Hey, Dad, the girls are really looking forward to meeting you," Andrew says with a smile.

Arnold smiles too when he hears 'Dad'. "I like the sound of that." He places his hand on Andrew's back and walks towards the rowdy uncles as they look at the photos.

Blake re-joins Dominic, watching the scene with a grin. "I think this is a happy ending, don't you?" Blake smiles and Dominic nods, wrapping his arm around Blake's shoulder.

"We've done our bit. We'll see them soon," he says. Blake smiles as Dominic waves at them, heading for the exit of the park. Ashley is carrying some paperwork and enters her office to start filing, when she notices Colin is sitting at her desk. On the table is a meal, sparkling water, and candles.

"What are you doing in my office?" she asks, trying very hard not to smile.

Colin stands up. "Having a date with the most special woman and baby in the world," he says with a smile. Ashley can't help but let a chuckle slip as her hand unconsciously strokes her stomach.

"You did this for me?"

Colin nods and smiles as he walks over and brings her into

a gentle hug. "Of course. I would do anything for you." He kisses her cheek, but it isn't long before the pleasant lunch is ruined by the racket of the office.

The noise that erupts is caused by Dominic entering the office, making demands. Blake watches in amazement. When Dominic glances towards him, Blake ducks and sneaks to his desk, starting to upload his pictures. Dominic can't help but smile. Colin smiles too as he watches Dominic gets back into his groove.

"Looks like the devil's back, which also means there are two tyrants in the office," Ashley says as she watches Dominic start typing like a mad man on his computer.

"Yeah, but that's what we wanted. He's finally out of his anger crushing ways." Colin nods as he adjusts his tie. "I better go give him a hand." He sighs as Ashley rubs his shoulder letting him know it's okay. With that, he goes back into the danger zone.

"Dom, what is going on?" Colin calls to him.

"I can finish the article," Dominic says, not taking his eyes off the computer screen.

"That great, how did it go with the reuniting of the son?" Colin asks. Dominic doesn't respond and Colin laughs when he sees the sentences appearing at a rapid pace on the screen.

Dominic comes to a halt. "Blake, have you got the pictures?" Dominic calls to him. Blake isn't responding either. Dominic stands up on his chair to look over the desks that separate them, only to find Blake isn't there. "Where is he?" Dominic asks. Colin shrugs.

Blake then steps out of the lift with coffees and food, "I thought we could use the fuel since the tyrant came back into action." Colin bursts into laughter at the comment.

A week goes by, and Dominic finally finishes the article. Ashley

134

looks over the article with the pictures of Arnold and Tallulah at stages of their life important to Arnold, the reunion of Arnold and Andrew, and a picture of Tallulah and Arnold dancing happily in the park. Ashley sheds a few tears as she reads the article. The last paragraph is about Dominic and Levi and their moment, and how, thanks to Arnold, Dominic has learned that in life, there is always a chance to make a new moment and cherish those already made.

Life is always about loving and being in 'a moment'. It's down to the moments created, no matter whether they were good, amazing, bad, or horrific. The future you build will always be better, thanks to those building blocks.

Ashley smiles and nods as she approves the article for the next issue.

As the article gets printed and sent out, Dominic sits at the café waiting for Blake and Colin to arrive. He watches people reading the article; some tear up at the story, while others read with a heart-warming expression. Dominic smiles as he leans into his chair, sipping his coffee.

Mrs M seated next to Dominic as Mr M brings them their drinks, Mrs M smiles as she finishes reading the article. "You did a good job," she says. Dominic can't say anything back. She gently kisses his forehead. "He'd be so proud of you." With that, she collects the empty cup and returns to the café.

Blake and Colin walk together with a newspaper in hand. "You're late," Dominic says.

Colin laughs, looking at his watch. "For what?" He shakes his head as he laughs slightly, and Blake continues to smile. "The article is a big hit. Everyone on the bus was talking about it."

Colin looks at Dominic who nods slowly. "That's good."

Mrs M soon greets them as usual from her seat next to

Dominic, her face lights up as she sees Blake and Colin join them.

Mr M carefully brings them their drinks as he shakily places the tray on their table. They all couldn't help but laugh and smile as they all looked at each other. And enjoy the good feeling that was spreading. Meanwhile at the elderly retirement home, Arnold sits at his usual table by the window reading the article. As his eyes dance across each of the letters on the pages, he smiles with each word.

"He's good," he says to himself. Chuckling, he turns the page over. Seeing more words and more photos of Tallulah and himself. He can't help but let out a satisfied sigh.

Suddenly an elderly gentlemen stands before him. His hat in his hands and gripped in front of his chest.

As their eyes meet, Arnold blinks in disbelief as he looks from one of the photos to the elderly man in front of him.

"David?" David nods as tears escape, Arnold carefully moves from his seat and embraces his friend.

"It's been too long," David says as he hugs him back.

Arnold and David played together all the way through childhood but were separated due to Davids parents splitting up.

Arnold pulled out a chair for David to sit with him.

As he did it wasn't long before they looked over the article and talked about back in the good old days and what they have been up.

While they do Arnold couldn't help but think that Dominic's article may have a hidden magic, bringing people together.

In Scotland Andrew looks around his breakfast his table as he excitedly reads the newspaper to his family, his children looking over his shoulder and looking at the pictures and pointing them out, listening to the stories.

"Who's he?" Laura asked, Andrew smiled as he looked at Arnold when he was younger.

"That there is my dad. Your grandfather." Andrew proudly said as he looked between the two. He looked to his wife who couldn't back the tears. He rose from his chair while his daughters looked at the pictures and article.

"I'm so happy, you found each other. You found him," she cried. Andrew pulled her into hug and gently swayed her as he sniffed holding in the tears that were threatening to breach again. It wasn't until his daughter sneaked in on the hug that he cried, happy tears.

"We're spending Christmas with them aren't we?" his wife asks Andrew nodded.

Laura giggled, "It's going to be the best Christmas ever, the biggest Christmas present ever is going to be meeting our uncles!" she smiled.

A year goes by.

Blake and Dominic are now dating properly. Colin has become a father, and has adopted the role of being a stay at home father. But on occasion crashes into the office just so he can show office his daughter, Natalia Moretti, Colin cried so when he was allowed to hold her, as soon as she was born, she became Ashley's and Colin's whole world.

Dominic has never been so happy for them. And jumped at the chance when they asked if he'd be her godfather.

Blake has been taking more pictures.

And even did a photo session for new family and Colin still raves at how beautiful they are. Blake has become a freelance photographer and is enjoying every second of it. He's also been featuring more in Dominic's articles which hasn't gone unnoticed. Dominic's been taking on more articles and is returning to his normal self, if not his better self.

Colin and Dominic keep in touch, mostly with pictures of Natalia, Colin sometimes writes the odd article about fatherhood. So much has changed over the year since the publication of the article. It's still viewed and used as an example for new journalists to get an idea of how to layout an article or the high standard most newspapers have for articles.

Dominic gets to desk after entering the office, he notices a letter on his desk. He notices the water mark that sits in the right hand corner next to the stamp.

"another letter," he tuts.

Out of curiosity, Blake picks it up,

"Why not open it?"

Dominic shakes his head and his eyebrow twitches slightly. "Because I know what it is." Dominic pulls out his chair and waits for his computer to load.

Colin laughs as he carefully rocks Natalia in his arms. "Oh, that again. It's a letter from the awards." Blake looks at them both excitedly. Opening the letter, he reads it out loud.

Dear Mr Wolf,

We're writing to you in regards about the award ceremony in honour of Levi Morstone. In addition, your article 'One Moment' has been nominated for an award. Inviting you to the evening to take part in the evening would be a great honour.

We would like to congratulate you and Mr Evans.

Yours Sincerely,

Writers Guild.

Blake looks to Dominic, who doesn't look all that interested.

Colin, on the other hand, looks at the letter while holding Natalia, a skill he has gotten good at. He sighs. "It looks legit, Dominic. You should consider it."

"Dominic, you should go, especially as it'll be my first joint award with you on an article."

Dominic sighs as he looks to them all. Even Natalia looks like she is giving him a pleading look. With a nod, Dominic turns back to the screen as he begins his new article. Blake jumps up and runs to his desk, then looks to Dominic. He had two letters.

"Wait, I have two." He opens the second one. After looking at the letter, Blake turns to Dominic. "It's a transfer letter to New York."

Dominic smiles and nods. "Well?" Dominic encourages him

"It seems like a massive opportunity. Something like this doesn't just come every day. I'll go," Blake says as he weighs the pros and cons, looking at the letter again. On the envelope is a sticky note in Dominic's writing: *I've been asked to go. I've said yes, but will you go with me?* Blake can't help but smile.

Ashley comes out of her office and there are stacks and stacks of boxes filled with letters. "Boys, that article you did had a brilliant response. Come take a look, will you."

Rolling his eyes, Dominic makes his way up the stairs to Ashley's office. Ever since the article, Dominic has been doing all sorts of articles and his image has returned to normal – with the odd one of course. Dominic has refused any interviews but insists that Colin takes them in his place with Blake, which makes Dominic all the more desirable for readers. They've tried sending letters, so Dominic has been doing a lot of walking back forth from Ashley's office.

Letters are displayed on the table, on the white board, and on the floor. Blake inspects them and smiles. As he does, he can't help but feel the warmth fill his heart at the comments in the letters.

"These letters are all for the article you wrote. It took the postal department almost a year to sort through them," Ashley says as she looks round the room, still in disbelief and amazement at how powerful words can be.

Colin, who sneaks into the room behind them with the push chair with a now sleeping Natalia, looks at the room in awe.

"Do you think you could do a follow up?" Ashley asks.

"Do a follow up? Heh, I'm back, aren't I? Let me see what I can do," Dominic says with a smile.

They all knew too well.

Chapter 12

Tallulah's eyes open before her alarm clock. The light travelling in through the window seems warmer and brighter than normal. She smiles as she reaches out to touch the rays. Her alarm finally starts to awake, playing the song 'I Lived'.

"What shall I wear today?" she murmurs to herself. She looks at the wardrobe that is wide open.

She slowly gets up out of bed, her steps slow and steady on the soft, bland, and beige carpet. The wardrobe has a small leaf design etched on the inside as she moves the door a little more, revealing more of her clothing. Her hand caresses the dresses and blouses that decorate the coat hangers, and she hums as she looks, picking one up and putting it back after inspecting it. She pulls one out, and her eyes sparkle as the colour of the dress is the perfect colour: a gentle rose pink.

The material is soft and stops at knees. The dress looks like chiffon but there is a silk feel to it with a cotton underlay, and a frill that is pleated up to the waist. The sleeves are short with a little pleat detail. She puts the dress against herself in front of the mirror and dances a little around the room. Satisfied with her choice, she picks her stockings.

Her jewellery is next. Tallulah picks a gold chain with her engagement ring on it. Her wedding ring still sits proudly on her finger, and she looks at it with a loving smile. Tallulah picks small pearls to go into her ears, and she looks at her shoes that are arranged neatly by her wardrobe. She decides to go for her black, small heeled shoes. After putting them on, she finds her white cardigan that stops just above her waist. She puts it on with ease, and for the first time in a long time she doesn't need assistance in getting ready. After checking herself in the mirror, she gently sits on the edge of the bed and waits for Emily to come and collect her. After all, it's Thursday.

Arnold lies in bed when he can feel a slight twinge in his heart. He thinks nothing of it and it goes away after a couple of minutes; to him it's nothing.

He is up like a jack in a box, picking a shirt and tie before Steven even enters the room. This time he wants to be the one to do it. He goes for the red tie with his white shirt, and a red and black square to sit in his jacket pocket. He picks odd socks because he always wore odd socks when he was younger, just like the day he met Tallulah. Humming a tune as he gets ready, he looks at his reflection and his eyes twinkle as he feels all the joy of recent events. He looks at his desk filled with new pictures of his grandchildren he recently met, pictures that now sit next to photos of Andrew and him. Arnold picks up a picture of himself and the grandchildren when they went to Jedidiah's house for Christmas, when they covered Andrew in silly string. Just beside the pictures is Mathew wrestling with Laura for the last sausage roll, as John picks it up in his fork. Another picture is of Lucy and Simon building a rocket ship under the close watch of John; another of Andrew and Arnold sharing a drink of whiskey as they watch the outside. There's even one of Simon and Matthew's kids all meeting Andrew. Each photo is cherished by Arnold, and he looks back to the one in his hand.

Chuckling at the memory, he smiles, stroking their faces. He loves them so much. A brown envelope sits next to the pictures. Picking it up, he places it on his bed. He opens it and flicks

142

through the pages, rereading the contents and nodding with each page. He's happy with what is on them. It's an updated version of his will, signed and approved by his lawyer. Arnold places it in his drawer. He searches another and picks up four keys; each key is labelled with a name. Placing them in the drawer with the will, everything is all together.

Arnold looks around his room, and everything seems to be vibrant with colour. He decides to take a stroll in the garden. As he walks, he places his hands behind himself, on the middle of his lower back, something he typically did. Taking deep breaths of the fresh air, he feels relaxed.

Arnold comes to a tree he likes, known as the winter flowering tree. Next to the tree is a person he has never met before, wearing jeans and boots with a simple shirt and a hoodie.

"Hello." the man speaks with a gentle smile. Arnold nods and sits on the bench just by the blossom tree. In front of it is a pond that has a few duck visitors.

"You must be Arnold?" the man asks.

"I am. And you are?" Arnold asks, looking to the man with a raised eyebrow

"Levi. I was just popping round to see a friend. You see, she's told me about you," Levi says, smiling. Arnold nods before looking at the pond. "Hadn't you better get going before you're late?" Levi asks Arnold.

Before Arnold can ask him what he means, Steven starts to call him. Arnold looks in the direction towards Steven and lets out a low groan as he slowly stands up from the bench. "Well, that's me. It was pleasant meeting you, Levi." Arnold turns around to find that Levi is no longer there. Looking baffled and slightly confused, he continues back to the home, thinking nothing of it.

"Wow, look at you," Steven says in amazement. "You look great," he says, looking at Arnold with a beaming smile. Steven shows him the usual basket and blanket and Arnold nods. Arnold shows Steven a book and some flowers that he is holding. "Is that a photo album?" Steven asks. Arnold nods at the question as he follows Steven to the car.

"Onward to see my one true love!" Arnold says, smiling to Steven who simply chuckles as he shakes his head. The car starts up with a beautiful low rumble, making the journey smooth and plentiful. The music in the background isn't noisy. It pleasantly lifts Arnold into happier spirits as he sings along, even if he is slightly off beat. He taps his foot and hand along with the beat. Arnold continues to look out the window as the view flashes by.

"Steven, have you asked Emily out on a date yet?" Steven looks at Arnold in shock

"What!" Luckily, Steven is stopped at a red light

"I think you two make a lovely couple," Arnold says, speaking each word with care. "Make your one moment. Don't wait too long, Steven, otherwise you'll lose it," Arnold warns him. Steven can't help but nod at the wise words Arnold has parted. Steven feels like he's on a mission, plucking up all the courage he has to ask Emily out.

It isn't long before the park is in view. Steven pulls up to the park and he spots Emily's car. "They're here," he says happily. Arnold smiles and nods as he opens the car door. Leaning backwards, he hooks his hand under his kneecap to pull his leg out, and eventually gets himself out of the car.

Steven grabs the things out of the car and looks to Arnold to see him grinning like a Cheshire cat. Steven chuckles as he walks over, shaking his head. He opens his wallet and pulls out a comb, handing it over to Arnold, who uses it to quickly brush his dishevelled hair.

"How do I look?" Arnold asks.

Steven nods. "Handsome as ever." Arnold nods back.

"I feel as if it's my first date every time I see her," Arnold says while gripping the photo album. He doesn't want to crush the flowers.

"You say that every time," Steven responds.

"Ah, that's because it's the truth," Arnold says with a smile, before straightening up and letting Steven know he's okay. Steven cautiously lets him go. Emily is waiting by the gate this time. Tallulah is just a little further on.

"Go get her," Steven chuckles.

Emily smiles, watching Arnold go to her. Kissing and hugging her, he compliments her on the dress. Tallulah does the tap and hold of his upper arm.

"They don't ever change, do they?" Emily comments.

Steven shakes his head. "No." He looks to her and bites the bullet. "Are you free this Saturday?" he asks. Emily looks away from them and blinks in shock.

"I am, why?" she asks, unsure.

"Go out with me?" Steven smiles at her. Emily can't help but smile with him and nod. "I'll pick you up at seven then."

Steven's phone buzzes with a text from Dominic that says he is on his way to see Arnold with Blake. "Oh, brilliant. Dominic is on his way," Steven chirps with smile. Emily looks over his shoulder and smiles.

Tallulah slips her arm through Arnold's arm. "Oh, Arnold," She sighs as she walks with him, "What a day," she says, looking around. Arnold joins her. He looks to where they sit; everything is set up.

"Tallulah, sit with me a moment." Tallulah stops walking

145

and nods. He sounds serious. "I have something important to tell you." She nods once again, listening. He opens the photo album, showing her Andrew and his family, and her eyes widen. Her hands shake as she touches the photos.

"This is Andrew Hall, our baby boy," he says, his voice shaking. Tallulah starts to cry as she looks through the pages. "He has a family of his own now, two children and a lovely wife. His wife owns a café and Andrew is a partner in a law firm. He's done so well for himself, and I couldn't be prouder of our boy." Tallulah stops looking through the pages and looks to him.

"He knows? He knows what happened?" He nods and she throws her arms around him and sobs into his chest.

Rocking her back and forth, Arnold continues. "I spent Christmas with Jedidiah, and they joined us." Arnold speaks with joy in his voice as he shares the stories with her. "There was so much laughter," he says. "Did you know Andrew changed his surname back to his original one, Hall, when he turned eighteen? His foster parents love him and didn't mind at all. In fact, they helped him through the process." Tallulah calms down, looks to him, and smiles.

"Our brave, baby boy." She kisses Arnold gently on the cheek and Arnold wipes her tear-stained face,

"How about that dance?" he asks her. She nods. Helping her up, they walk to where the musicians are playing, and gently sway with the tune and song.

They twirl into the days where their memories aren't fogged or chained away. Where the dance halls are filled with bunting reaching from one end to the other, where the smell of the rose garden mazes fill their noses. The strokes of the petals under their fingertips as they walk past them, and the feel of the cold rain on the last night of the carnival. The first time they saw an opera show and the first time they sat together on a sofa in a home that they bought for themselves. Each memory they shared and cherished floods before their eyes with great care and love, seeing the loved ones before them, smiling and waving to them and watching as they dance in the memory of those days. Twirling, they see the smiles of Tallulah's and Arnold's parents on their wedding day. Tallulah smiles as she looks at Arnold, his young, handsome face looking back at her and the love in his eyes making her so happy. Arnold slows down and kisses her cheek.

Taking Tallulah's hand, Arnold plants a gentle kiss upon her wedding ring and takes her back to the bench. The memories surrounding them fade once again.

Steven and Emily are watching from the café with Kyle as they finish their dance and return to the bench, their heads resting on each other whilst wrapped up in the warm, ruby red and sapphire blue flannel blanket.

Dominic comes into the park and jogs over to the café. "Hey, you guys. How's it going?" He greets them and Emily nods and smiles. Dominic raises an eyebrow and chuckles. "He finally asked you out?" She nods and Kyle sips on his coffee, when Steven reacts.

"What do you mean, *finally!*" he asks in astonishment. Dominic laughs at his reaction. Blake finally catches up, slightly panting.

"You're fast." Blake puffs. Dominic smiles and kisses his cheek.

"No, you're just sweetly slow." Dominic looks over to where Arnold and Tallulah are sitting. "I'll wait here and go over when they're about to head off." Steven looks at him then back to them, crossing his arms slightly.

"You sure?" Dominic nods.

Tallulah sighs slightly. "Arnold."

"Hmm?" A tired response is given.

"What is he like? Andrew, I mean." Tallulah sounds equally as tired.

"He reminds me of you. He has a bit of me and a bit of your dad, but he's lovely, kind, polite, and caring. He's going to do well," Arnold says.

"We'll watch over him and his moments." Tallulah hums her response. "I love you," she whispers.

Arnold holds her hand in his, under the blanket. A gentle sigh escapes his lips. "I love you too," he whispers softly.

Chapter 13

Some time passes and Dominic starts to feel uneasy. "Something isn't right." He gets up from his chair and runs over to the bench, skidding to a stop in front of Arnold and Tallulah.

"Arnold?" he calls to him, giving him a slight shake. It isn't long before Steven is behind him, bumping into him.

Steven places his two fingers on Arnold's wrist, then on Arnold's neck. "No pulse. He's gone. We need to call an ambulance and the home." He looks to Tallulah. Emily and Kyle are right behind them. Dominic begins to move Arnold when Steven stops him. "they have a do not resuscitate. We can't do anything." Dominic looks at him in shock. The words coming from his mouth were like a bucket of cold water.

"Arnold. No he didn't" Steven nodded at Dominics words as they came out in a small pleading voice.

Emily was already on the phone with emergency services. Kyle wiped a tear from his eyes and sniffed. Putting a glove on his hand, he held Tallulah's hand.

"She asked for someone to hold her hand until her body is taken away by the ambulance," Kyles voice is unrecognisable.

Dominic watched for a few minutes before looking to Blake.

Dominic is immediately brought into a hug by Blake and taken away from them. It isn't long before the ambulance arrives, taking them away together carefully. As they place them in the back, their hands fall slightly as if they are still looking for each other.

Dominic wraps Blake up in another hug. Emily cries into Steven's chest, whose tears fall down his cheeks. Kyle cries into Steven's shoulder, leaning on him for support.

Watching the ambulance leave is Levi in a hoodie, standing a little way away before disappearing behind a tree.

As Steven gets to the home, he makes his way into the nurse's office, picking up the phone as it weighs heavily in his hand. As the phone dials, Andrew picks up.

"Hello?"

Steven can't say anything at first, then he clears his throat to speak. "Mr Hall? It's Steven." Steven speaks carefully, which is unusual for him, and Andrew notices.

"Steven. What happened?"

Steven sighs heavily into the phone. "Arnold's condition worsened, and he had a minor heart attack. His heart gave out." The phone was silent.

Andrew falls into his chair. Staring at the photo of him and his dad, his heart sinks. He opens his mouth to say something, anything, when Laura enters the room. Seeing Andrew on the phone she gently pulls the phone out of his hand.

"Hello, this is Laura." Steven sighs as he pulls the phone away.

"Hello, Laura, can I talk to your mum please?"

Laura answers with a nod and finds her mum. Passing the phone over, Steven explains what happened and ends the call. Andrew quietly sobs in his office as his wife enters slowly, closing the door behind her.

"He's gone," is all Andrew can say.

Steven stares at the phone when the head nurse enters with a cup of tea. Sitting next to him, nothing is said between them. There is a gentle silence as he stares at the other numbers he still

150

has to call.

A week later and the whole world knows about the death of Arnold and Tallulah Lovelock. Describing them as 'lovely, with fabulous personalities', Dominic and Colin publish an article about it all.

"Don't waste any 'one moment'. Cherish them all – past, present, and future ones. They're special because they guide you in every way," Dominic reads out. "Arnold was a wise old man. Cheeky, stubborn, and smart. He taught me things I never knew I could do." Dominic looks out to everyone in the church. Every seat is filled with people wearing colourful clothes and each person nods with every words Dominic he speaks says, some are clutching their tissues.

"Arnold taught me that a smile is better than a frown, a dance is better than a fight, and that joy is friends and family pushing you through the mud that catches you at the ankles. Friends and family are something I thought I didn't have much of, but he taught me I have lots of them. To listen and hold onto them. I owe my thanks to him." Dominic starts to choke as he looks at the crowd.

"He made the decision to ask for help. He placed his precious one in a specialised care home. The strain he had on his heart emotionally day in, day out seeing her forget everything about herself, him and those that surrounded them. It's heart breaking for anyone to go through. Let alone Arnold. Arnold even though he struggled with this decision he knew it was the right one. Arnold was a private man, so no one knew he had a heart problem, but he wasn't one to share problems. He was one to take them and fix them with the strength he possessed. The brave thing he did is admitting to himself he needed the help, and he got what he needed. Arnold entered the Sunset Pearl Home

151

and Tallulah went to the Hedgehog Care Hospice to get the specialist care she needed. And that she got. In confidence, Arnold told me that Tallulah was the one who told him it was okay. It was okay to let her go. The bravest thing he ever did was to ask for help and Tallulah is so proud of what he did for her. For them. For being brave. But he wished he'd been there for her. I don't think he realised he was. So, when he discovered that one day a week, she remembered him. Arnold savoured every second of it, thanks to the nurses and carers of the homes that worked together to make that happen." Dominic nods to Steven, Kyle, and Emily, who are all red eyed.

Andrew is holding his children's hand, surrounded by Tallulah's brothers, who are now his extended family. "Apparently he had asked that I talk at his funeral. I couldn't believe it at first but, like always, Arnold was stubborn and he got his way. It is a great honour to talk about Arnold. An amazing man, wonderful family man, and a spectacular friend, I mean, he could have asked for anyone better to talk for him. I'm never good at this part." There is a small chuckle through the church.

"We've lost two beautiful souls, but heaven has gained them and I know that they'll be watching over us. I can hear Arnold demanding a nice cider, and Tallulah asking for a dance." Dominic sighs as he coughs a little. "I think I've said enough now." Dominic steps down and returns to his seat. Colin and Ashley are sitting with him and Andrew nods to him in thanks. The rest of the funeral continued.

It isn't long before they are outside watching the coffins placed side by side. Tallulah's brothers each hold one of Andrew's and his family's hands as they stayed.

One by one, people leave. Blake notices that Dominic is stood by a different grave, and the priest is stood with him.

"He's looking at his previous lover's grave."

Blake turns to where the voice came from. Levi. But to Blake, he has never met this man before. Levi stands by his side wearing a hoodie, in the light, drizzly forecast.

"Previous?" Blake asks.

"You know the photographer," Levi says as he watches Dominic exchange words with the priest

"Oh, Levi." Blake says, sounding sad as he realised what he meant. "He was – is – someone I look up to," Blake says, sounding happy and sad. Levi smiles and pats Blake on the shoulder.

"You know he loves you very much, right? Dominic."

Blake looks from Levi to Dominic and nods. "And I loved him from the moment I bumped into him and spilled water all over him. It was like a bolt of electricity went through me," Blake says, trying to explain.

"Good, take care of him for me. Well, not for me—no, that's not the right word. Take care of each other. I'm glad you chose each other." Levi begins to walk further into the wooded area and Blake calls out to him.

"Hey, what's your name?"

"Levi Morstone."

"Levi Morstone. No way. Wait! Hey, you can't go out that way, it's a dead end…" Blake starts to drift off. When he follows him, he finds that no one is there. Instead, there is a sudden rush of wind that gently wraps around him.

After the priest has left Dominic's side, Dominic looks up and watches the trees rustle. Blake wanders over, placing his hand into his.

"Everything okay?" Blake asks as he looks from Levi's grave to Dominic.

Dominic nods. "Yeah. Just told Levi that I found someone as promised, and I asked the father to look after the grave for me." Blake stares at Dominic, who kisses his forehead and pulls him into a hug. "Ready to go?" Dominic asks. Blake nods and smiles as he looks to Levi's grave.

"Are we all ready to head to New York now?" Blake asks him with a smile and loving gaze. Dominic smiles back and nods, gently squeezing him.

"Yeah."

Blake grins as they leave the churchyard, looking forward for their new moment to begin.